Dead Broke

Center Point
Large Print

Also by Vannetta Chapman and available from
Center Point Large Print:

Deep Shadows
Joshua's Mission
Raging Storm
Sarah's Orphans
Light of Dawn
What the Bishop Saw
When the Bishop Needs an Alibi
Who the Bishop Knows
Dead Wrong
Anna's Healing

**This Large Print Book carries the
Seal of Approval of N.A.V.H.**

AGATHA'S AMISH B&B
Book Two

Dead Broke

An Amish Cozy Mystery

Vannetta Chapman

CENTER POINT LARGE PRINT
THORNDIKE, MAINE

This Center Point Large Print edition
is published in the year 2021 by arrangement with
the author.

The text of this Large Print edition is unabridged.
In other aspects, this book may vary
from the original edition.
Printed in the United States of America
on permanent paper.
Set in 16-point Times New Roman type.

ISBN: 978-1-64358-904-6

The Library of Congress has cataloged this record under
Library of Congress Control Number: 2021930322

Dedicated to
Priscilla Wright

While this novel is set against the real backdrop of Hunt, Texas, the characters as well as the community in Hunt are fictional. There is no intended resemblance between the characters in this book and any real members of the Amish community. As with any work of fiction, I've taken license in some areas of research as a means of creating the necessary circumstances for my characters. My research was thorough; however, it would be impossible to be completely accurate in details and descriptions, since each and every community differs. Therefore, any inaccuracies in the Amish lifestyles portrayed in this book are completely due to fictional license.

Glossary

Bruder—brother
Dat—father
Danki—thank you
Dawdi Haus—grandfather's house
Englischer—non-Amish person
Fraa—wife
Gotte—God
Gotte's wille—God's will
Grandkinner—grandchildren
Grossmammi—grandmother
Gut—good
Kapp—prayer covering
Kinner—children
Mamm—mom
Nein—no
Ordnung—unwritten rules of the community
  (literally "orders")
Rumspringa—running around time
Schweschder—sister
Ya—yes
Youngie—young adult or teenager

"There is a way that appears to be right,
but in the end it leads to death."
PROVERBS 14:12

"I have learned that to be with
those I like is enough."
WALT WHITMAN

Chapter One

Agatha Lapp sat at the patio table with her new guests, Henry and Emma. The couple looked to be in their sixties, were celebrating their second anniversary, and hailed from Colorado.

"Not many Amish there, I imagine."

"Indeed. Monte Vista and Westcliffe are the two largest communities—and they're small by anyone's standard." Henry smiled mischievously. "Not everyone agrees with our liberal ways."

"Henry is teasing," Emma clarified.

Emma was round and motherly, and Agatha had taken an immediate liking to her. Henry, on the other hand, was slim with a white beard and hair more gray than brown that curled at his collar. He was the bishop of his community. Emma had confessed that she'd never envisioned herself being a bishop's wife. They'd both laughed at that.

"We're not actually liberal, but we do have solar power." Emma tucked a stray hair into her *kapp*. She wore the traditional Amish dress and apron, but the dress was a pretty russet color and the apron ivory. "Many Amish communities do these days—even traditional communities."

"*Ya*, it's so." Agatha glanced back at her house, which sported a good-sized solar panel on the roof. "We've always had it here in Hunt—solar energy was approved by our bishop and deacons when the community first was formed a few years ago. But I also had some Plain guests last week from Shipshewana, and they tell me nearly every house there has a solar panel now."

Henry picked up his glass of iced tea and ran his fingers along the top edge. "You probably know more about the Amish than I do, Agatha."

"Doubtful." The wind momentarily picked up, causing her to pull her sweater more tightly around her shoulders and temporarily snatching her attention away from the conversation. She turned back to Henry and Emma, picking up the threads of the conversation. "We do have guests from all over—both *Englisch* and Amish, but I only know what they want me to know. You're a bishop. You know secrets."

"But you're a kind woman with a listening ear. I would imagine that as a bed and breakfast owner, folks confide in you on a regular basis."

"I'll admit that some days I feel like an Amish Dear Abby."

They all laughed, and Agatha had the passing thought that rarely was an afternoon so perfect. She did enjoy being a B&B owner, though guests weren't always as affable as Henry and Emma. Some were picky, others were exhausted, and a few simply couldn't be pleased. Agatha some-times wondered if that last category had their visit paid for by relatives who needed a week without them. It was an uncharitable thought, but eighteen months running a B&B forced you to see the world through realistic glasses.

Still, this day was like something from a storybook. The river sparkled below them. The temperature had risen to a pleasant seventy-four, though it was cooling now. Agatha was grateful for the sweater she'd brought outside with her. Storm clouds had rolled in and rain was predicted for early evening. It had misted earlier in the day, but hardly enough to make a difference in area water levels. They could always use rain in the Texas Hill Country.

"Oh, here comes Tony." Agatha stood and waved, then felt ridiculous doing so. Of course he knew she'd be in the garden. She loved spending the last hour of the day watching the birds and deer and assorted wildlife. An old chicken coop had marigold flowers and monkey grass spilling from it. Brick pavers, a birdbath, a bench, and a special bronze plate dedicating the place to her brother decorated the space. She'd recently added a small wrought iron table with four chairs.

Tony arrived, smiling and apologizing for his clothes—his pants had water stains up to the knees though they looked as if they'd dried at least. Agatha thought her neighbor grew more handsome every day—black hair tinged with gray, a trim build, and brown eyes and skin.

After she'd introduced everyone, Agatha asked, "Did you have a good day on the river?"

"Wonderful, actually. We lucked into some largemouth bass. I believe the Hochstetlers enjoyed their time fishing the Guadalupe."

"The Hochstetlers are also staying here for the week," Agatha explained. "Tony acts as a fishing guide when anyone needs him."

Tony laughed. "It's a tough life, but someone has to do it. Beats my old job, that's for certain."

"What did you do before?" Henry seemed genuinely interested. "If you don't mind my asking, that is."

"Not at all. I was a detective with the Hunt Police Department for thirty years."

"Detective and sergeant," Agatha added.

Henry and Emma exchanged a look, her eyes widening. He reached for her hand and covered it with his own. Now what was that about?

"Interesting work, I imagine."

"Yes. While you see the worst of people, you also see occasional acts of kindness and charity that you wouldn't expect. I enjoyed the work."

"But you enjoy fishing more?" Emma cocked her head and studied him. "Or do you miss the work?"

"Some days I miss solving cases, chasing bad

guys, puzzling through the clues. Most days I enjoy the fishing more."

"Does this mean we're having fresh fish for dinner?" Henry asked.

"*Nein.* We encourage catch and release, which ensures a healthy population for the next fisherman." When Emma looked at her with a raised eyebrow, Agatha added, "It's strange the things you learn when you live on a river."

Suddenly the pleasantness of the afternoon was broken by the sound of a car backfiring. Agatha wondered if the new neighbor next door was working on his late model cars again. Tony glanced up sharply at the sound and looked out toward the road. His eyes met hers, and then he shrugged. As the car noise faded, it was replaced with that of frantically bleating goats.

Agatha turned to Tony. "Are Nathan's goats still clearing across the river?"

"They were when I paddled past them early this morning."

"Goats? Clearing? You lost me." Henry twisted in his chair to stare at the river, then turned back toward them. "Which is another reason I love to travel. I always learn something new."

"Nathan King is a member of our community who hires out his goats." Now that Agatha was paying attention to the sound, those goats sounded like they were in quite a panic. "Since they'll eat nearly anything, it turns out they're good for clearing areas, especially slopes with poison ivy."

"The land across from Agatha is owned by a youth camp," Tony explained. "They've been intending to clean up their river frontage for some time, but it's difficult to do when campers are there running down the slope and jumping into the river. November's the perfect time."

"The goats certainly sound upset." Emma craned her head in the direction of the river. "Sounds almost like babies crying."

"That they do." Agatha scowled. Crying babies were not conducive to relaxing afternoons for vacationers. "Do you think something's wrong?"

"Let's walk down and check." Tony stood, then held out an arm for Agatha.

She looped her hand through the crook of his arm, marveling at how natural it felt. She wasn't exactly sure of her feelings for Tony Vargas. They could probably best be described as *complicated*. He'd suffered the death of a spouse, the same as she had. But he was also a retired detective—a very *Englisch* thing to be. That had come in handy when a guest turned up dead on her property a little over a year ago. She ran straight to Tony's house next door, though she'd barely known him then.

A close friendship had blossomed from those difficult times, and maybe something more.

Amish folk didn't marry outside their faith, not

that Tony had proposed. But if he did, he would have to convert. She couldn't imagine him being Amish. He drove a large truck, carried the newest cell phone, and was a practicing Catholic.

A romantic relationship would be problematic.

She did know that she was grateful for his friendship. He'd helped her out of more than one difficult situation. He was the reason she wasn't sitting in a Texas jail at the moment. Never mind that, he was the reason she was still alive. She shook her head.

"Problem?" he asked in a low voice.

"Just remembering all we've been through together."

"Yup."

Which pretty much summed it up.

The little group made their way down to the river frontage. Henry walked with a cane, though he didn't seem to depend on it too heavily. Emma had mentioned that he'd had a knee surgery a year or so ago. They walked a few paces ahead, oohing and awing at the beauty of the Guadalupe River that bordered the back of Agatha's property.

Instead of ceasing their commotion, the goats were bleating more loudly than ever. By squinting her eyes, Agatha could just make them out across the river. They were all bunched up on the side of the hill.

"Something's definitely wrong." Tony glanced

at Agatha, then added, "I'll paddle over and check it out."

"Let's all go." When he looked at her in surprise, she nodded toward her guests. "Emma and Henry both said they enjoy time in a kayak."

Henry nodded and Emma clapped her hands. "I love a good adventure before a soaking rain," she said. "At least those clouds look like rain."

"We could use it too after the dry summer we've had." Agatha stared up at the clouds. "We should be back before the first drops hit the ground."

Tony began turning over kayaks.

Henry helped fetch the paddles and life jackets, and within five minutes they were paddling across to the opposite side of the river.

Agatha's weather prediction skills were terrible. Big fat drops of rain began to hit the water before they'd even pulled up to the far bank, and the sky had turned noticeably darker. A northerly wind whipped Agatha's *kapp* strings back and forth, so she pulled them to the front and tied them together with a loose knot. It felt as if the temperature had dropped a good ten degrees since they were sitting in the garden.

"This way." Tony led them up a deer trail.

It was only a moderate slope, but with the raindrops increasing and the wind picking up, Agatha felt as if she were struggling to climb a mountain.

The goats continued to bleat—their voices

sounding like the impatient cry of a dozen children. Agatha again caught a glimpse of them through the trees, all bunched up. They weren't grazing. They weren't doing anything but crowding one another this way and that. What had scared them?

Agatha was directly behind Tony, so she noticed the moment his back stiffened. He stopped and held up a hand like a traffic cop. Behind her Henry and Emma skidded to a stop. It was only when she peeked around Tony that she saw a shoe, then a pants leg.

Her mind began to spin, telling her she couldn't be looking at what she was plainly looking at.

"Is that a man?" Emma asked.

And then Henry was saying, "Stay with Agatha. Tony and I will check it out."

Agatha and Emma shared one look, then followed the men. Agatha liked that about her guest. Emma wasn't one to sit back and wait, and God himself knew that Agatha didn't tend to either.

But she wasn't prepared for the scene spread out before her when they drew closer.

Goats bunched up, heads raised high, bleating in a chorus of cries.

Tony rushing forward to kneel beside the body.

Henry looking left, then right, then joining Tony to offer his help.

And Nathan King?

17

Nathan King was lying on his back, eyes wide open, arms spread wide, staring up at the sky, and not seeing a single thing.

Nathan King was dead.

Chapter Two

O nce they'd determined that Nathan was long past any first aid assistance, Tony pointed to a spot twenty feet away. "Stay under those trees. They'll provide some protection from the rain."

He used his cell phone to call the police while Henry, Emma, and Agatha huddled together.

Trying to stay dry.

Trying to calm the goats.

Hoping they hadn't stomped over any and all clues from the crime scene—and it was a crime scene. The hole in Nathan's chest confirmed that. But she hadn't heard a gunshot.

Had she?

Agatha nearly slapped her forehead when she remembered the car backfiring. Of course it hadn't been a car. Why had she thought that? Why had she assumed that? And would Nathan still be alive if she'd acted more quickly?

Agatha blinked her eyes rapidly and ran her fingertips up and down her arms. She was suddenly cold, much colder than five minutes ago. Her teeth had begun to chatter, and she clamped her mouth shut.

It was shock. That's what it was.

Nathan King was dead.

She'd said hello to him at their last church meeting. He'd stopped to share a funny story about his goats.

Why would someone kill him?

Who would do such a thing?

The light rain had turned into a downpour by the time the police arrived and took control of the crime scene. Tony said something to the officer in charge, pointed across the river, and then nodded toward Agatha. The officer stared at the ground a moment, hands on his hips, shook his head in disbelief and then nodded once.

It was all Tony needed.

He hurried over to where they stood waiting. "We can go. Officer Barella will send someone to come and take our statement when they're done here."

The group turned to stare at the officer in charge. Barella was rather short and stocky with a buzz haircut. He didn't wear a hat or a raincoat. In fact, he seemed oblivious to the fact that the Texas skies had opened up and unleashed a real gully-washer of a storm.

"Are we to paddle back . . . in this?" Agatha could barely see her place across the river, the rain was falling so hard.

"Nope. I'll fetch the kayaks for you tomorrow. Officer Griffin has offered to give us a ride back."

Agatha thought it more likely that Tami Griffin would escort them into the back seat of her police cruiser, lock the doors, and cart them off to the Hunt Police Department. They had a shared history, Agatha and Officer Griffin, and it wasn't a good one.

The group picked their way up the hill to the police cruiser and climbed inside. They'd barely started down the road which led to the bridge that crossed the Guadalupe before Griffin started interrogating them.

"Seems like people die around your place quite often, Agatha."

"That's not fair, Officer Griffin." Tony was sitting up front next to her.

Agatha, Emma, and Henry were in the back. Agatha couldn't help wondering when the back of the cruiser had last been cleaned. Was that a speck of vomit on the seat back? Surely not.

"I'm just saying. It's a pretty rare thing to have a dead body pop up in our little town." Griffin turned down the volume on her police radio. "Agatha had one in her cabin and now there's another directly across the river."

Agatha mouthed, "I'll explain later," to Emma and Henry.

Tony attempted to distract Griffin by discussing the particulars of the current case. "With this rain, it's doubtful they'll be able to gather much evidence."

"Convenient," Griffin muttered, as if Agatha might have caused the storm.

"What will happen to the goats?" Agatha hated to think of them in the rain, frightened, their owner and caregiver dead.

"A local veterinary clinic has offered to round them up and board them until something else can be worked out." Griffin turned onto the bridge, crossed it, then turned back toward Agatha's place. "This rain is bad enough, but those goats probably ate any evidence we might have found."

Was that the murderer's plan? Had he waited until Nathan was among the goats to kill him? Had he waited for the storm? And who would want to kill Nathan King?

Agatha briefly closed her eyes. She was not getting involved with this investigation.

Emma was speaking in a low voice to Henry. Agatha caught the words *evidence* and *clues* and *drawing,* which made no sense at all. Henry only patted his wife's hand and whispered that they'd talk about it later.

They rode the rest of the way in silence. When Officer Griffin dropped them off at the circle drive of Agatha's B&B, she reminded them, "Don't leave town. Don't go anywhere. An officer will be here to take your statements in the next hour or so. Tony, I'm holding you responsible to make sure she stays here until we get that statement."

Tony didn't respond to that. Instead he thanked her for the ride. Agatha appreciated that Tony didn't feel the need to defend them. Where would they go? And how? Speed off across Texas in her buggy pulled by her sweet mare Doc? Tami Griffin had been watching too many crime shows, or maybe she was simply bored with issuing speeding tickets, which was the extent of the crime in Hunt, Texas. That and illegal drug possession—something Agatha didn't even want to think about.

She led everyone up the steps and hurried them inside. The sky had turned darker, rain continued to lash the ground, the wind was now buffeting them from the north, and she felt suddenly chilled. Agatha's yellow cat Fonzi lay on the living room floor, pausing as he meticulously cleaned his paws to scrutinize the group. Unimpressed, he went back to licking his paw, then wiping it against the side of his face. She'd inherited the cat with the B&B and was determined that it remain an outdoor cat, but Fonzi hadn't quite adapted to her plans.

"Will it be all right if we go to our room and change?" Henry asked. They were staying upstairs in her nicest suite.

"*Ya.* Of course. Gina will have dinner ready soon, so come down after you've freshened up."

At the mention of her name Gina strode into the front room. Gina Phillips had recently turned

23

fifty. She had short gray hair and the body of a long distance runner, though she laughed outright when anyone asked if she participated in marathons.

"You won't catch me running unless you find a bear behind me," she told the last guest who'd asked. "Even then, I'd only have to run faster than Agatha, which would amount to a medium walk. She's even less athletic than I am."

Gina had started out as a housekeeper, but now she helped run the B&B. She was efficient, hardworking, and quite outspoken. She was also one of Agatha's closest friends.

"You're dripping on the floor. All of you are." She handed them towels that she'd grabbed from the laundry room. "Did you really take those kayaks out in this weather? I saw you walking down there and couldn't believe you meant to actually—"

"There's been a murder." Agatha used the towel to wipe off her arms and face.

"What? Again?"

Agatha dearly wished everyone would quit saying that. It wasn't like her B&B was murder central.

"I need to make a few calls." Tony pulled his cell phone from his pocket and stepped back out onto the front porch.

"We'll be back down in a few minutes," Emma said. "Dinner smells *wunderbaar*."

"Texas chili, fresh cornbread, and salad, with Dr Pepper cake for dessert," Gina called after them. When they were out of sight, she rounded on Agatha. "Are you serious about the murder? Who's dead? And how did you end up in the middle of it?"

"I need to change clothes. Come with me, and I'll fill you in on all the details."

Ten minutes later, she had on fresh clothes and was sitting at the table. The Hochstetlers, oblivious to what had happened, were already seated, though Joey Troyer was absent. Agatha hadn't actually seen the man all day. He'd checked in rather early, spent less than ten minutes in his room, and then he'd taken off, claiming that he meant to spend the day fishing.

He didn't ask to borrow fishing poles and tackle so he must have brought some with him. Agatha wasn't sure. In fact, she hadn't actually seen him arrive or leave.

It had certainly been a long and traumatic day. Surprised to find she had an appetite, she hopped up to help Gina put dinner on the table.

Henry and Emma sat upstairs, having donned fresh clothes and collapsed onto the two over-stuffed chairs that faced the darkened windows. The rain continued to pound against the window-panes, but the room was warm and cheery with cozy battery-operated lamps lit throughout.

"I can't believe this is happening again, Henry. What are the odds?"

"Low. Definitely low." He studied his wife. Emma had saved him, in more ways than one. She'd been a friend to him when he sorely needed one, and now she was so much more than a friend. Her smile was the first thing he saw in the morning. Her body snuggled against his was the last thing he felt at night. Having a wife—having a helpmate—was still a new and wondrous thing after so many years alone.

"Are you frightened?" He tapped his fingertips against the arm of the chair. "If you'd rather cancel the rest of our stay here, I'm sure Agatha would understand."

"*Nein*. Not at all."

"*Gut*. I'm looking forward to some bird watching."

"Long walks along the river."

"Sipping coffee in the garden."

Emma nodded vigorously, then turned her gaze to the window, staring out at the darkness. "It is unusual though. Three murders in Monte Vista in the space of three years, and now this."

"A sad state of affairs."

"For sure and certain it is, and terrible that it would happen across from such a lovely B&B. I like Agatha. Don't you?"

"*Ya*. She seems to be a genuinely kind person."

"Though I'd like to hear the story of a dead guest showing up in her cabin."

"Indeed."

Emma turned in her chair, positioning herself so that she could study her husband. "You can help. You know you can."

"But should I?"

"Of course you should. You heard what that nice detective said.

"Tony . . ."

"He said the rain will have washed away any evidence."

"No doubt."

"So you'll do it? You'll draw what you saw?"

Henry stood, as did Emma. She stepped into the circle of his arms, and Henry reveled in the smell of her, the comfort of her there next to him. How God had blessed him these last few years— all of his life, really. He hadn't always been able to see it. Even his *gift,* as Emma liked to call it, had been a blessing from God. He understood that now.

"I'll help if I can." His voice sounded tentative, even to himself.

Indulging his unusual ability had never been easy. It sometimes caused more problems than it solved. Emma had helped him embrace it, but still he understood that not everyone responded well when they saw what he could do. In Monte Vista, at least he'd had the support of his congregation behind him. Here, no one knew him, and no one would understand or believe him. At least he didn't think they would. There was a 50/50 chance they'd write him off as some kind of eccentric old man.

But maybe he needed to try.

Agatha seemed like a kindred spirit for certain, and even Detective Tony had been affable. Perhaps God had placed them here, at this time, for a reason.

"Let's go down and eat. You must be starved."

"I am, and I'm not sure I've ever had Texas chili." Emma slipped her hand in his and they made their way down the stairs.

The bed and breakfast was quite amazing— old, yes. In need of updating, perhaps. But it had the feel of home to it, and wasn't that a special surprise when one was vacationing in a distant land? Henry was glad that Emma's son had insisted they take a vacation. It really was so interesting to see how other communities within their faith lived. He'd been surprised to learn that the price of the room included breakfast and dinner.

As they took their seats at the table, Tony walked in.

"I've set you a plate, Tony." Gina pointed to the end of the table.

Tony looked as if he was about to protest, then apparently decided better of it. Gina seemed to have a persuasive way about her. Henry's *mamm* had been like that. It was usually easier to do what she asked than to argue.

He was surprised when Agatha cleared her throat and said, "It's our practice to pray silently before a meal. Since you all are Plain, and Tony's a frequent guest, I'm sure I don't have to explain."

In the moment of silence that followed, something inside of Henry clicked into place. While it was true that they were in a different place, among people they barely knew, and once again involved at least peripherally in a murder investigation—God was still in control.

A chorus of *amens* were heartily offered up, and then the dishes were passed around. Gina joined them once she was sure everything that could possibly be needed was on the table. Agatha and Tony took turns explaining what had happened across the river, catching everyone up, and explaining that the police would stop by later to take their statements.

"We went straight to our rooms after you dropped us off, Tony." Daniel Hochstetler offered a worried half-smile. His hair was a pure white, and his shoulders slumped. Overall, he looked to Henry like a man who needed a vacation. "I might be seventy, but I didn't expect a day on the river to wear me out. We actually took a nap before dinner."

"I could barely keep my eyes open," Mary admitted. She wore Amish clothes similar to Agatha and Emma's. "Perhaps that's because I'm more used to knitting than rowing."

Henry noticed a slight tremor in her hand as she reached for her water glass. Gina passed around the crock of butter. "This butter is made by one of Agatha's Amish friends. You be sure and try it on the corn muffins. And Tony, I can vouch for the Hochstetlers. They came in at four-thirty, right after Agatha went outside to sit with Henry and Emma."

"Seems everyone here has a solid alibi then." Tony meant it as a joke, but no one laughed.

An alibi.

Most people didn't need an alibi while they were on vacation.

Henry cleared his throat. "So this Nathan fellow, he was a member of your church, Agatha?"

"*Ya*, he was. I still can't believe he's dead." She reached for her glass of water, took a small sip, and returned it to the table. "Nathan was in his mid-fifties, and he never married."

Gina scoffed. "What woman would put up with those goats?"

"You're not wrong." Agatha stirred her hot bowl of chili, then added a bit of shredded cheese to the top and took a bite. It tasted like cardboard to her. Why would it taste like cardboard? Were her taste buds in shock too? She noticed Gina studying her, so she smiled and said, "Delicious."

It was a small lie. She silently prayed for forgiveness.

"Well, you don't pay me to cook bad meals."

Agatha turned her attention back to Henry. "Nathan did love those goats. We went to dinner once, and it was all he could talk about."

Tony nearly choked on his chili. "You dated Nathan King?"

"I'd hardly call it a date. We went to dinner at Sammi's."

"Sammi's is the best place in Hunt to eat," Gina explained. "Their cooking is almost as good as mine and Agatha's."

"But why would someone kill him?" Agatha's face paled, as she carefully set her spoon down and slumped back against her chair. "It's so hard to imagine a person doing such a thing, planning it and then carrying it through."

"Not all murders are premeditated," Tony pointed out, reaching for another cornbread muffin. "He could have made someone angry. It's quite possible it was a spur of the moment thing. There was an argument say, and the guy . . ."

"Or gal." Gina shrugged when they all turned to look at her. "Women are capable of murder. Remember that case six months ago? In San Antonio? The woman learned that her husband had another family. She waited for him to come sneaking home like an old tom cat and hit him in the back of the head with a shovel."

No one knew what to say to that.

Tony cleared his throat. "Okay, so a man or woman becomes angry for whatever reason, takes off, fetches their gun, comes back and shoots Nathan. My point is that it's not necessarily someone who had it in for Nathan for a long time and planned it. Often homicides are the result of emotions careening out of control."

Henry thought of the time young Albert Bontrager had tried to hitch a new horse to his buggy—a horse that even the previous owner had claimed was too wild to be of any use. Albert had trained the gelding, eventually. But there had been many madcap rides through the Monte Vista countryside. For several months, if you saw a cloud of dust, you could count on it being Albert with his wild horse.

Henry's mind was filled with that memory, and he felt an itching to draw it. Albert, the wild horse, a swirl of dust obscuring and confusing everything. He could draw it and name it *Homicide*, because as Tony pointed out, the out-of-control emotions were much the same.

"It's incomprehensible," Agatha practically whispered.

Gina scoffed. "There's no figuring out people, Agatha. But Tony's right about one thing. It could have been that someone was angry with

Nathan and went to the youth camp specifically to murder him. Everyone knew Nathan was working that stretch of the river with his goats. There was even an article in the paper about it."

Tony sat back, sipping his iced tea and staring at a spot on the far wall. "Recent studies show that fifty-three percent of murders are committed by someone the victim knows."

"Terrible." Emma's voice was low and troubled.

"Twenty-four percent of murders are committed by family members."

"Cain murdered Abel," Henry reminded them.

To which Daniel Hochstetler added, "Someday the scales of justice will be perfectly balanced."

"Not today though." Agatha took a small bite of the chili, then pushed it away. "Today we mourn the passing of a friend, a *gut* man, and a neighbor."

And then their meal was interrupted by a knock on Agatha's front door. Officer Barella had arrived, and he was ready to take statements.

It was two hours later when Henry and Emma climbed the stairs to their room.

They'd each been taken into the living room separately to give their testimony. Tony had assured them this was normal, that it helped to not cross-contaminate the testimony. When he'd started to explain what that meant, Henry had lifted his hand to stop him. He understood. He'd been through this before.

Though he didn't share that fact, not yet.

And when his time came to give his official statement, he also didn't share with Officer Barella what his mind knew. After all, he didn't know what his mind was aware of. It didn't work that way. Instead he told what he'd heard and what he'd seen, which really hadn't been much.

Henry and Emma readied for bed. She pulled out a little bit of knitting she liked to work on before sleeping. She'd explained to him after they'd first wed that it helped to calm her thoughts. "I know we should pray. I do pray, but the knitting . . . it makes that easier too."

He'd nodded as if he understood, which he didn't, having never knitted anything himself. But he loved other things that had the same effect—watching sunsets, studying birds through his binoculars, drawing.

One of the first gifts Emma had given him was a drawing journal. Now he pulled it from his suitcase along with several pencils, kissed his wife, and sat down at the small desk.

Pulling in a deep breath, and praying that God would use the work of his hands, he opened the journal and he began to draw.

Chapter Three

Agatha awoke feeling much better than she had the night before. Nathan's death was a tragedy—for sure and certain it was. But it didn't involve her. She had a bed and breakfast to run, and she'd focus on that. The Hunt Police Department could handle the murder of Nathan King. Perhaps they'd even call in the famous Texas Rangers to solve the mystery. What was certain was that they wouldn't be needing the help of an Amish *grossmammi*.

She smiled at that thought.

Although all of her *grandkinner* were in Indiana, the oldest, Marcus, had already come to visit her in Texas. She would go to her son's over the Christmas holiday to see everyone, and perhaps more of the *grandkinner* would travel from Shipshewana to spend time with her the following summer.

It was with those cheerful thoughts filling her mind and a hymn on her lips that she made coffee and sat on the porch with Fonzi. The morning was quite cool, and the land felt freshly scrubbed from the storm the evening before. After she'd finished her first cup of coffee, she moved inside to put both the pecan streusel and breakfast quiche in the oven. She'd just shut the oven door when Henry and Emma walked into the room.

"I hope I didn't wake you with my rummaging around in here."

"Not at all," Henry assured her as Emma headed straight for the coffee pot.

While Emma looked rested, there was a furrow to her brow that hadn't been there before. And Henry, well, Henry looked exhausted.

Concern for her guests replaced all other thoughts. Had her small flock of guineas landed on the roof above their room? Guineas were gangly animals and made a terrible noise, but they were good at keeping the snake population in check. She'd purchased a half a dozen earlier in the year. They roosted each night in the trees at the back of the house, but occasionally they also dropped down onto the roof. "You didn't sleep well?"

"I did, for a few hours." Henry accepted the cup of coffee from his wife, then they both sat down across from Agatha.

It wasn't unusual for her guests to rise early, especially her Amish guests. After all, the majority of them were farmers, used to rising before the sun tiptoed past the horizon in order to care for horses and cattle, goats and pigs. Since Henry was a bishop, he carried the work of a farm plus the duties of a church leader . . . though he had shared that they lived with Emma's son in a *Dawdi Haus*. The younger man did the majority of the farm work.

Still, she'd never had anyone join her for coffee at five-thirty in the morning.

"What's wrong?"

"There's something we need to tell you, Agatha." Henry looked at his wife.

Emma nodded emphatically before adding, "And something we need to show you."

Henry pulled in a deep breath and blew it out. Looking up at her, he gave a tentative smile. "I was injured, when I was only twelve."

Agatha sat back, interested, but wondering how something that happened so long ago could cause him such worry now.

"I was playing baseball that day—the day that changed my life—and my friend, Atlee, he was up to bat. Atlee had a powerful swing. I turned sixty-seven this year, but I can still remember that day as if it just happened. The sun shone brightly in the sky, and the temperature was warm. The leaves in the trees were just beginning to turn."

He stared out the kitchen window, and though there was no tremor in his voice, Agatha felt a chill creep down her spine.

"I even remember the sound the ball and bat made as they collided with one another."

Henry sipped from his coffee. It seemed to Agatha that he did so more to give himself time to collect his thoughts than out of a love for the drink. She suspected that Henry had slipped into the past, and he was no more aware of the coffee in his mug than he was of the Texas hills outside the window.

"The impact was to my skull." He touched a place on the side of his head. "I was taken to a hospital, where they drilled a small hole to reduce the pressure on my brain."

She couldn't imagine such an impact. How terribly painful it must have been. "But you recovered," Agatha said.

"I did. They called it a catastrophic brain injury. My condition stabilized rather quickly. I went home, and I lived a rather normal life."

"Except for the drawing," Emma murmured.

"Yes, except for the drawing." He sat up straighter and locked gazes with Agatha. "Some doctors called me an Accidental Savant and others said that the injury caused Acquired Savant Syndrome. The names are synonymous to me and beside the point. I was suddenly able to draw, completely and accurately, anything and everything I had seen."

"He doesn't remember all those things, mind you." Emma smiled at her husband. Had she told Agatha they'd been married for two years? Agatha would have guessed they'd shared an entire life together, and perhaps they had—a lifetime could be calculated in so many different ways.

Henry watched Agatha carefully. She wasn't sure what she was supposed to say. She couldn't think of why he was sharing this event from his past with her.

"My unconscious mind remembers, and I'm able to draw scenes people and places and things down to the smallest detail."

Agatha tilted her head to the side. "That's what you were doing last night?"

"*Ya.*" He again sipped the coffee.

"And you were drawing . . ." Her thoughts tossed about, trying to put together Henry's story from his childhood with anything that could have to do with her. And suddenly Agatha understood, or she thought she did. "Oh . . ."

Emma jumped to Henry's defense. "He doesn't do it all the time, mind you. He doesn't want to intrude on people's private moments. It's been hard, this gift that Henry was given, but it's also . . . well, it's brought some unsavory characters to justice."

Agatha felt her heartbeat kick up a notch. "You've been involved in a murder investigation before?"

"Three times in Monte Vista and once in Goshen."

Agatha shifted in her chair, suddenly remembered the food in the oven, and jumped up to check on it. She set her wind-up timer for ten more minutes, and returned to the table. "So you have a photographic memory?"

"*Nein*. No one has that, or so the doctors say. My conscious memory is the same as anyone else's. It's my subconscious that records and is able to produce the images."

"Okay. And last night you . . . what did you do exactly?"

"Last night I drew what I saw on the far side of the river. I drew Nathan King's murder scene."

It was then that Agatha noticed he'd placed a spiral journal on the table next to where he sat. He picked it up, turned to a page in the middle, and passed it to her.

Agatha thought she had understood what Henry had told her, but when she looked at the drawing, a gasp escaped her lips. She'd seen plenty of photographs before, though in general Amish didn't own cameras or have their pictures taken. There were exceptions in the last few years it had become quite common for a bride and groom to have their picture snapped a few times. Nothing like hiring an *Englisch* photographer and staging a photo shoot, but a few mementos for the couple that they could keep or share with family.

The drawings before her were like that.

What Henry had drawn, it resembled a photograph more than a drawing.

It contained such detail that she leaned forward to catch the smallest things, then she sat back and held it at arm's length. "This is amazing, Henry. It looks . . . it almost looks as if it could jump off the page, as if it isn't flat at all but rather a physical model of the thing."

"There's more." He nodded at the journal. "Turn back."

So she did, first one page, then two, then a third. He'd made four drawings in all, and she had the sense that she was looking at a time-lapse video.

"How can you do this?"

"Technically—well, technically no one can explain it, and I certainly don't understand. It has something to do with the brain injury though. I couldn't . . ." He ran a hand across his brow, pausing to rub above his left eye. "I couldn't draw stick figures before I was hit with Atlee's baseball."

Emma stood up, snagged the coffee pot, and refilled their cups. Agatha immediately liked the woman even more than she had the night before. Emma saw a need and filled it, and at the moment Agatha desperately needed more coffee.

The timer dinged, and she removed their breakfast from the oven, covering both dishes with a clean kitchen towel to keep them from cooling too quickly. Gina would arrive soon. The Hochstetlers would come to breakfast, and perhaps Joey Troyer would show, though Agatha hadn't heard him come back to the B&B. He must have, though. Where else would he have spent the night?

She had two more couples checking in, and she'd meant to work on a quilt she was making for a couple at church. Plus, visitation would begin with Nathan's family. She knew his parents though only casually, and there was a younger brother the one who would probably take Nathan's goats. Nathan hadn't talked about his family nearly as much as he'd talked about those goats.

Like most days running a B&B, this one was going to be busy. But all those things she had to do faded as she again scanned through Henry's drawings.

Finally she raised her eyes to theirs. Henry and Emma were worried. About what? About the drawing? Why would that concern them so much? It didn't implicate them in anyway. And yet it did involve them, and perhaps those other investigations hadn't gone well. Perhaps they weren't eager to again become involved with the *Englisch* police. It was a basic tenet of Plain life that they strove to live alongside other people and faiths, but still set apart.

With these drawings, Henry was walking right into the thick of things—right into the middle of the Hunt Police Department and a criminal investigation. And he was doing it because he knew that what his mind had seen could help solve the murder. Her respect for the couple seated across from her increased even more, and it had been considerable to begin with.

Agatha reached across the table and squeezed both Emma's and Henry's hand. "We'll show these to Tony. He'll know what to do."

Because Tony Vargas might be retired, but he was still the finest detective in the state of Texas.

Henry and Emma decided to take a walk along the river before breakfast.

"Agatha was surprised." Emma reached for his hand.

"*Ya*, but not frightened by what she saw. I'll take that as a good sign."

So instead of worrying over what might happen in the next few hours, they watched the sun rise over the hills, sending rays of orange and pink across the Texas sky. They were even treated to the sight of several fish jumping out of the water and slapping back down, causing water and light to spray across the surface of the river.

"Nickel for your thoughts." Emma bumped her shoulder against his, drawing him out of his reverie.

"I thought it was a penny."

"Yes, but your thoughts are worth immensely more to me."

Henry nodded toward the river and the hills beyond. "I was thinking that I'd like to draw that."

"It's beautiful."

"Perhaps I could take up landscapes instead of murder scenes."

"No doubt they would sell better."

They'd never tried selling his drawings. They'd talked about it, but Henry didn't want the attention it might bring. Whatever money could be earned wasn't worth that trade off. But perhaps there was a way he could do so through a third-party, and the funds would certainly help their family as well as their congregation.

"Interesting how Agatha thought immediately to share them with Tony."

"She trusts him." Henry picked up a smooth flat stone and skimmed it across the water, feeling like a child again. It was a good feeling—clean and fresh and filled with optimism. "They've been through something similar together, as she hinted at last night. She trusts his reactions as well as his instincts."

"Then we will too." Emma smiled broadly.

It was that simple with her. Put your trust in the good people, step away from the bad ones. And she definitely knew how to discern one from the other. They both did.

The truth of it was that Henry was tired of drawing scenes of the worst that one man could do to another. He'd thought he was done with that, and yet here it was again.

He did believe that God directed his steps. He'd

spent as much time praying as he had drawing through the long sleepless night. Because he didn't understand why this was the cup he must drink from once more.

But he did understand his duty.

They'd eat breakfast with Agatha's other guests, and then they'd take his journal to Tony.

An hour later they were sitting in Tony's kitchen. He offered them coffee, but Henry thought he might begin buzzing if he had any more. Instead, he asked for a glass of water.

"Henry needs to show you something," Agatha explained. "It's about Nathan's murder."

"Okay." Tony drew the word out, like a long piece of taffy.

So Henry again told the story of his injury, but this time he added the reactions he'd dealt with each time he'd dared to show someone his drawings.

"My parents were the first to see what I could do. I was just fiddling around, drawing people from a church social, wishing I could be outside playing instead of inside recuperating. I drew our friends and neighbors. I didn't realize that I had caught some of those people in an unflattering light."

"Such as?" Tony wasn't actually taking notes, but Henry had a feeling the man forgot very little when he was interviewing someone regarding a murder.

"A man speaking unkindly to his wife, two boys fighting, a teenaged boy about to kiss his girlfriend." Henry cupped both hands around the glass. "It wasn't so much what I drew as it was the . . . the intensity of it."

"It was intrusive."

"Yes. It was." Henry felt his head bobbing, surprised that Tony had understood what he was trying to say. "As if I had an *Englisch* camera and was taking pictures of people when they weren't aware, when they thought they were alone. My parents told me that no one wants their every action and emotion recorded. They called it a curse, this unusual ability of mine, and they strongly suggested I never draw again."

"But you did?" Agatha looked riveted by the story, even though she'd heard the first part earlier that morning. Now she was hearing it after having seen for herself what he could do.

"Not for a long time. There was a murder, in Goshen, and I thought—I knew—I could help find the killer of a young Amish girl—Betsy Troyer."

"You did help find her killer." Emma tugged on her *kapp* strings so hard, Henry thought she might tear them. "Remember, I was there, Henry. You suffered mightily when they arrested you, but in the end you're the reason that Gene Wooten didn't kill again."

"All right." Tony sat up straighter. "I'm

beginning to understand why you might not want to jump into a situation. Your ability somehow makes you suspect."

"Exactly. It's as if I know things that I shouldn't be able to know, unless I was complicit."

Tony was already shaking his head. "That's not possible this time. I was with you, before, during, and after Nathan's murder. So the worst that happens is someone will think you're a bit unbalanced mentally."

Emma was quick to defend him. "Henry's the most stable person I know."

"There were three more murder investigations, in Monte Vista, that I found myself caught up in," Henry said. "On at least one occasion, I needed an alibi and I didn't have one. Things were . . . tumultuous for a while. The police eventually caught the killer, though."

"All right. Warning issued and received. Let's see what you've got there."

Henry, Emma, and Agatha exchanged a look.

Then Henry passed the journal to Tony.

Tony didn't speak at first. He studied the drawings, glancing more than once at Henry. Then he stood, fetched a glass of water, and gulped downed the entire thing. He remained there at the kitchen sink for a moment, staring out across his backyard that, like Agatha's, sloped down to the Guadalupe. Finally, he returned to the table and smiled at Henry.

"I thought I was ready for that."

"Indeed . . ."

"I was raised a Catholic, still am a Catholic, I suppose." Tony smiled a bit apologetically. "Mostly I find God out there . . . on the river, but my mother, she made sure I understood and appreciated Our Lady of the Lourdes, the Shroud of Turin, even The Holy Face of Manoppello. Catholics—we're not skeptics as far as believing in miracles goes, and this . . ."

He tapped the journal. "This is a miracle."

He ran his fingers down the edge of the page.

"My point is that I don't doubt what you've done here. More importantly, I think there may be some very important clues."

"I thought so too," Henry murmured.

"Let's take it one page at a time. It looks to me as if you drew them in chronological order."

"Yes, the first is when we ascended the hill and saw the goats and the man's body."

Everyone leaned forward to study the page that Tony had opened the journal to, though Henry and Emma were looking at it upside down.

"Here we have the goats—in amazing detail. Probably not much use to the investigation though."

"Look at this goat. There seems to be some sort of fibers or . . . something . . . around his neck." Agatha looked at the others. "Any idea what that might be?"

No one had a guess at all, though Tony complimented her fine powers of observation. He turned to the next page. "Here we have Nathan, arms spread wide, lying face up, after he'd been shot through the chest. I suspect what you've drawn will mirror the photographs taken on scene."

"*Ya*. I imagine so."

"Remember the rain began as we were crossing the river. The evidence surrounding the body was being erased as we made our way up the hill, but still there was more there when we arrived than when the police did. So let's look at what might have been erased in the fifteen minutes before the Hunt Police Officers took control of the crime scene." He pointed to a spot beside the body. "Here's a small scrap of paper. You only drew a corner of it, why?"

"Because that's all I saw. It was crumpled, like you see in the drawing. My mind can only reproduce what my eyes actually saw—there's no guesswork. That corner was all that was visible."

"I don't even remember it, and I'm fairly sure it wasn't there when the police arrived, so the rain must have washed it down the hill. But we can just make out the words *pay for what* . . ."

"Most bills aren't handwritten, so it's not that." Agatha crossed her arms, curiosity coloring her features. "And why was he holding it in the middle of the woods while he was tending to his goats?"

Tony shrugged. "Possibly it was a note someone left for him earlier. Maybe he'd stuck it in his pocket and his hand brushed against it— remembering, he pulled it out."

"Or maybe someone threatened him, then killed him," Emma said.

"Why threaten him, though? Why make yourself known?"

"Because they wanted something?" Henry understood that the reasons for murder were varied, and sometimes—to a sane and balanced person—there seemed to be no reason at all.

"Let's move on." Tony pointed to the bottom of the drawing. "Here you have the heel of a boot print."

"It's in the next drawing too."

"It had rained a little that morning, barely a mist actually. I remember because I was relieved to not have to water my potted plants." Agatha cocked her head, studying the drawing. "It looks as if the ground was wet enough to retain the print."

"Even on dry soil you can sometimes find footprints. This . . . it's a fine print even though it's partial, and even though the rain was beginning to erase it."

"You can use that?" Emma asked.

"Possibly. Boots in these parts are often custom

made, and that means that the soles are original; plus, each person wears the tread on the bottom of their shoes in the same way. Go to your closet, turn over all your shoes, and you'll find similar patterns of wear on the bottom. This is good. It's not a complete print, but it's enough that the police could do an analysis on it."

"The question is, will they." Emma frowned at the journal. "Often they are skeptical of Henry's drawings."

"Having been a detective, I can understand that. We're trained to question everything we see. These drawings? These are like receiving a gift . . . they're pretty much too good to be true."

"But they are true," Agatha reminded him.

"We know that. I can't guarantee what the investigating officer will think though." He indicated the bottom right corner of the drawing. "There's also a tread mark here. It's just a partial tread, and like the boot print it could be from days or weeks before the murder, but . . ."

"Do you think it shows how the killer arrived?" Emma asked.

"A person who is committing murder will often remember to pick up their shell casing, but they rarely remember that they leave impressions in the dirt with their shoes and possibly with their mode of transportation."

"Too many trees to be a tire track," Henry pointed out.

"For a vehicle, yes. But if it were a mountain bike . . ." Tony peered more closely, then shook his head. "Let's look at the next drawing."

The first drawing was from a distant viewpoint. The group had approached the body, which was why it had included the goats huddled nearby. The second was drawn from the perspective of Henry and Tony as they'd knelt next to Nathan. The close up of the man was disturbing, to say the least.

Nathan was Amish. He was dressed in a blue shirt, work pants, and suspenders. He'd been wearing a straw hat, but it had fallen to the side of the body.

"What can you tell me about Nathan, Agatha?"

"He's roughly our age, I guess. Hard worker. Single. I don't know much else."

Henry thought the man seemed a bit unkempt—his hair needed a cut, and it didn't look as if he'd shaved recently.

"The victim was shot and fell onto his back. He hadn't been moved at this point. The bullet either went through his body or it was lodged inside. Look at his neck though."

They all leaned closer to the drawing, so that the tops of their heads were practically touching.

"Looks like some light bruising." Agatha's voice contained the confusion Henry was feeling.

"Do you think it was recent?" Emma murmured.

"Looks to be, in this drawing. If so, there might

be some DNA from the person who left the mark. The Medical Examiner will check it out, I'm sure. But it could mean that whoever shot him approached him first. Perhaps they had an altercation, a little push-shove-choke."

"The ground is undisturbed around him," Henry noted. "And Amish don't push or shove. They certainly don't choke one another assuming the person who killed him was Amish. We don't know that of course."

Tony let that go. He did note, "There's only the single boot print. Our perp didn't hop over, grab Nathan around the neck, then hop back and shoot him."

"This all seems like risky behavior to me." Agatha leaned forward now, elbows resting on the table. "Whoever did this wasn't thinking very clearly."

It occurred to Henry that if he had to go through this again—go through yet another murder investigation—he was glad to go through it with Agatha Lapp and Tony Vargas.

"Why would a killer leave a note?" Agatha shook her head, a quick jerk left then right. "Why would he choke Nathan?"

"Our list of questions grows." Tony turned the page to the third drawing. "Remember, I'd moved you three over to a nearby stand of trees."

"To get us out of the rain." Emma offered Tony a quick smile.

"Right. So it's as if we're getting a broader view of the area here."

"The body looks the same to me," Henry said.

"It does, but you've drawn more of the area behind the victim."

Agatha sat up straighter. "The area the bullet would have gone, if it isn't still in him."

"Yup." They all four hovered close to the photograph, the tops of their heads practically touching.

"There." Henry tapped a tree near the top of the drawing. "It's a very small spot, but I think . . ."

Instead of answering, Tony stood and walked into the adjacent room that he used as an office. He returned with a magnifying glass and held it over the portion of the drawing they'd been studying.

"Do you think . . ." Agatha's voice now held a note of wonder.

Henry didn't even remember drawing the detail, but there was a small hole in the bark of a tree. He might have thought an animal had caused it except the hole was perfectly round.

"I don't know if that's the bullet or not, but it'll be easy enough to check." Tony turned to the last page of drawings.

"I believe that's as we were leaving," Henry explained. "As you can see, it's again from a distance, and I recall I had looked back over my shoulder."

It was quite apparent from the drawing that the police had taken over control of the crime scene. Some were kneeling by the body, others were wrapping crime scene tape around adjacent trees, but one was standing apart and looking not at the body of Nathan King, but at Agatha's group of friends.

And the expression on Tami Griffin's face? It could only be described as a look of suspicion.

Chapter Four

After asking for and receiving Henry's permission, Tony took the journal back into his office and copied the relevant pages. He returned the journal and thanked him for sharing it. "You didn't have to become involved. Given your history with law enforcement, I wouldn't have blamed you if you'd kept this to yourself."

Henry and Emma shared a look.

Agatha understood it to mean that they'd talked about it, considered staying out of the investigation, and probably prayed about it as well. In the end, they'd done what their conscience had dictated.

"You'll take it to the police?"

"Yes, and they'll probably be in touch with you."

Henry nodded, as if he'd expected as much. He thanked Tony for his help, reached for Emma's hand, and they made their way back toward Agatha's property.

Tony tugged on Agatha's arm as she started after them.

"Talk to you for a minute?"

"Of course."

"What do you think?"

"About Henry? I think he and Emma are *wunderbaar* people. What do you think?"

"I think I'm a little freaked out and trying not to show it."

"Because of his drawings."

"Yeah. Have you ever seen anything like that before?"

Agatha shook her head.

"Can you . . . I don't know . . . check out his story?"

"You want me to check up on Henry?"

"Just float some questions out there. Didn't you tell me once that you have an Amish grapevine?"

"*Ya.* I suppose I might have said something like that."

Agatha laughed for the first time since hearing Nathan's frantically bleating goats. The poor things. They must have been frightened out of their minds. If only goats could speak . . .

"Say, that reminds me." She worried her bottom lip, then plunged into what she needed to say. "When we were sitting at the table, before we kayaked across . . . I thought I heard a car backfire."

Tony was nodding before she'd finished. "I heard it too. Figured it was someone sighting in their gun for deer season."

"But if I had realized what it was, maybe . . ."

"No." The look he gave her was filled with

such tenderness that it brought a lump to Agatha's throat. "You couldn't have saved him. I couldn't have saved him. Nathan was dead before he hit the ground. It happens that way sometimes."

"Okay."

Tony clumsily patted her shoulder, then crossed his arms. "So you'll ask around? About Henry?"

"Sure. I can check with my bishop, or possibly my friend Becca. I think she once told me that she had relatives in Goshen. They might remember Henry from his time there." She rubbed a finger along her bottom lip, then added, "I'm from Shipshewana myself, which is a short buggy ride from Goshen, but of course, I was busy raising children then. Still, I don't remember any talk of a murder or of a bishop who had an extraordinary talent for drawing."

"I'm pretty sure anyone who has met Henry . . . anyone who knows what he's capable of . . . will remember him."

Agatha followed Tony over to his pick-up truck. He apparently felt it was important to take these drawings to the police right away. She didn't understand the hurry. Nathan would still be dead, and she suspected his killer would be lying low.

"Why are we checking up on him? I can't see that Henry would have any reason to lie, and the drawings . . . well they sort of speak for themselves."

"Agreed, and yet detectives question things. It's a habit that dies hard."

Agatha reached out and patted his shoulder. She'd become increasingly familiar with Tony, and she was fast adjusting to the Texas way of doing things. Soon she'd be pulling complete strangers into a hug and offering them large glasses of sweet tea.

"Thank you, for not laughing at him."

"I would never."

"And for helping."

At this he stepped closer and lowered his voice. "Promise me you'll stay out of this, Agatha."

"Stay out of it?"

"I'll turn the drawings in to Lieutenant Bannister. Hopefully he'll send someone out to speak to Henry, and then that's the end of it."

"After I make a few discrete inquiries."

"Yes, after that."

He returned her smile, and she felt her heart race a little. Tony was one suave guy, and he was endearing too. A ball cap covered his thick crop of black hair that was just beginning to gray. He wore his standard uniform—blue jeans, a plain t-shirt, and a blue jean jacket. It was hard to believe that a little over a year ago she'd barely known him. A little over a year ago, they'd been involved in another murder investigation.

He stepped back and crossed his arms. "Just remember, this isn't a mystery like those books you read."

"Who has time to read?"

"I saw them in your living room."

"For the guests."

"And one on the kitchen counter, with a scrap of yarn for a bookmark."

"Caught me."

"I'm not kidding. We're not getting involved. This isn't like last time. This isn't about you or your property or your guests. We're going to help the investigation by giving Henry's drawings to the authorities, and then we're going to wash our hands of it."

"Absolutely right." She moved to the edge of the driveway, then waited for him to back out. Once he'd pulled out onto the main road, she gave him a little wave and headed across the lawn to her place.

A row of hedges marked the property line, and there she turned and looked back at him. Tony had yet to drive down the road. Instead he sat there, truck idling, watching her. Was he waiting to make sure she got home safe? She waved again to indicate that she was fine, that she could traverse the great distance of a few hundred feet without any mishaps, and then she turned back and walked through the hedge.

She heard Tony's truck head toward town.

And then she heard a scream, coming from the B&B.

Agatha broke into a run.

By the time she reached the back porch steps, she was out of breath. Mary Hochstetler had dropped into a rocker, her face pale and her hand pressed against her heart. Daniel stood beside her, assuring her that everything was fine. And Gina? Agatha's friend and housekeeper was standing three feet away, having picked up a quite large rat snake with the end of a rake.

"Don't usually see these in November," she admitted. "They're harmless of course—in fact, they're rather helpful. They keep the rodent population down. I better relocate him to the garden."

She trotted off without another word.

Daniel continued to console his wife, who looked quite shaken.

Agatha sat in the rocker next to Mary. "Are you all right?"

"Yes. I suppose. It just . . . it gave me a fright is all."

"That's understandable. The first time I saw a rat snake I was sure it was a rattler. I was about to attack it with a hoe when Gina stopped me."

Daniel had fetched his wife a glass of water. She took it in trembling hands and attempted to take a sip, but the water splashed onto her lap.

"Are you sure you're all right?"

"*Ya*. It just gave me quite the fright."

She didn't look all right. She looked as if she might faint, even with the snake safely moved to the other side of the property.

"I believe I'll go to our room and rest for a few minutes."

When her husband moved as if he meant to go with her, she waved him away. "I just need to lie down, Daniel. I'm fine. Go ahead and do your fishing."

Agatha and Daniel watched her totter into the house.

"I'm sorry about that," Agatha said.

"Well you can't be responsible for the wildlife as well as everything else." Daniel cleared his throat, then added, "A few months ago, Mary had a scare with a diamondback rattlesnake at our place. I believe she may be developing a phobia."

He picked up the fishing pole he'd dropped and made his way down the path that led to the river, then turned left and meandered down the bank.

Which left Agatha sitting there, wondering if everyone was hiding something. Because the Hochstetlers were from Ohio, which was not a common habitat for diamondback rattlesnakes.

He'd either lied about the snake or he'd lied about being from Ohio. But why would he do that? Or was he simply confused? Perhaps he was developing early onset dementia. She didn't know, but she filed the question away in her mind, thinking that she would mention it to Tony later. At some point she was going to have to start writing these things down. There was only so much a B&B owner could be expected to remember.

One look at Tony's grim expression told Henry that the police would not be coming to interview him.

Tony found him sitting in an Adirondack chair, studying the river.

"Where's your better half?"

"An apt expression if there ever was one. Emma is inside helping roll out pie crusts. It would seem that you can take the woman out of Amish country, but . . ." He waved a hand to indicate that Tony probably knew the rest. "Have a seat. I take it you have bad news."

"So you think they laughed at me and threw me out?"

"It crossed my mind."

Tony sank into the chair next to him so that both men were facing the river. "They laughed at me and threw me out."

"I can't say I'm surprised, but thank you for trying, Tony."

"He barely looked at these." He tossed the envelope with Henry's drawings on the table between them. "Jimmy Bannister is the lieutenant for the Hunt Police Department. He isn't a bad detective, but neither is he known for thinking outside the box."

"Those . . ." Henry nodded at the envelope. "Are definitely outside the box."

"Yup."

"So what do we do?"

Tony shook his head. "I don't know. I was a detective on the Hunt PD force for many years, but I retired a few years ago, when my wife was sick. Camila died not long after Agatha bought the B&B. I still miss her, still expect to see her in the kitchen when I come down in the morning, or in the bed reading a book when I give it up for the night."

"I'm very sorry for your loss." Henry understood the pain and grief that came with the loss of a spouse. It had been twenty-eight years since Claire had died, and he now understood that the hole left by a loved one's absence never fully closed. You learned to live with it. If you were fortunate, you even learned to laugh and love again—as he had with Emma—but you never stopped missing that person you lost.

"*Muchas gracias.*" Tony sat back, clasping his hands together. "After Camila died, I didn't adjust well. The job was gone, and then my wife was gone. I guess I had trouble finding my place again. Agatha helped me with that."

"You two seem like good friends."

"We are." Tony glanced over his shoulder at the

64

B&B, then back at Henry. "She's a special lady, that's for sure. I haven't quite figured out if we're just friends . . . or something more."

It wasn't the first time Henry had heard this sort of thing. He was after all a bishop, and as the Amish community intermingled more with the *Englisch*, it was bound to happen that the occasional man and woman from different backgrounds would be attracted to one another.

He'd learned it was best to keep his opinion on such relationships to himself. Most people worked out what was best for them . . . what God intended for them. It was only when they specifically asked for his opinion that he gave it, and Tony was not doing that. He was once again staring at the river and reflecting on the path his life had taken.

"I always thought I would enjoy retirement," Tony admitted. "I didn't expect to feel at loose ends."

"The trouble with doing nothing is, it's too hard to tell when you're finished."

Tony nodded vigorously. "Exactly. Anyway, when Agatha was involved in that incident last year, it felt natural to step back into my old role as detective."

Henry didn't have to ask. Tony offered a quick recap of the murder of Russell Dixon.

"Now I'm tempted to do it again, in spite of the fact that I told Agatha we shouldn't get involved.

But if the Hunt PD won't follow up on a solid lead . . ."

He picked up the envelope, though he didn't pull the pages out. Henry suspected he didn't have to. He remembered well enough what he'd seen.

"The boot print was good. They could have followed up on that . . . should have."

"Is there anything we can do?" The question popped out of Henry of its own volition.

Now Tony turned to him, an embarrassed grin on his face. "I've put in some calls to local boot makers."

"Smart."

"There's one more thing." Now Tony sat forward and readjusted his cap against the mid-afternoon sun. "What's really bothering me is that bullet. If it's where your picture shows it is . . ."

"Should we go and check?"

Tony nodded, first slowly and then more vigorously. Finally he turned to Henry. "Are you game?"

"Fish aren't exactly biting."

"You don't have a rod."

"Could be the problem."

"Take the kayak?"

"Yes." Henry realized he was curious. He didn't question what he'd drawn, but that didn't necessarily mean they were interpreting it correctly. If they found the bullet, and if it could lead the police to the murderer, it was worth an hour of his time.

Fifteen minutes later they'd paddled across the river and climbed up the slope. The ground was still slick with mud from the rains the day before, but the crime scene tape was gone.

"They finished up gathering evidence this morning," Tony explained.

It wasn't hard to find the spot. If you'd known what you were looking for, it was easy enough to make out the outline of where Nathan King had died. Tony pulled out the drawing, and they stood there at the foot of Nathan's outline and studied the picture.

"Lots of trees."

"Probably why the property owner decided to use the goats. It's hard to control vegetation along a slope and amongst trees. As you can see . . ." he pointed to a clump of brightly colored foliage—all with three leaves per cluster. "The poison ivy had become pretty thick in here."

"Not the best thing to have around large groups of young ones."

"Exactly." Tony thrust the envelope and drawings into his hands. "Let me know if I get off course."

What followed felt like a child's game to Henry. Two steps, move forward, three to the right. Now go straight. Left. No, back a step and left again. Surely he had played something similar as a child, and standing under the live oak trees on a beautiful November day, the memory made Henry smile. Even in the midst of a tragedy such as Nathan King's death, there were bright moments, and Henry had found one.

"Here it is," Tony called.

By the time Henry reached his side, Tony had pulled out his cell phone and taken a few pictures. Staring at the tree bark, Henry saw the end of something shiny—the end of a bullet, no doubt, though who could tell how long it had been there.

Tony tapped a few buttons on his phone and waited.

"We found the bullet. It was where Henry said it was, where he drew it."

Henry could make out the other man's voice . . . argumentative and clipped.

"I'm sending you the picture. If the perp was standing downhill from the victim, the bullet would have traveled through Nathan and up. The bullet would have traveled exactly where we found it."

He hung up on the call and pushed a few more buttons. Almost immediately his phone dinged and he received an answer. He typed in a reply and returned the phone to his pocket. "A forensic team is on their way."

Chapter Five

Agatha had a busy afternoon. It was a little after lunch when she checked in Patsy and Linus Wright. They were recently retired, lived in Houston, and looking forward to some time in the "peace and quiet of the country," as Linus put it. Agatha didn't dare mention they'd just had a murder across the river. The Wrights would hear about it soon enough. No doubt Nathan's death was the talk of the town, though one could barely call Hunt, Texas a town.

Another hour passed as she finished early preparations for the evening's dinner. Sometimes she cooked, other times Gina did, and occasionally they worked together in the kitchen which resulted in some excellent Southern Amish dishes. In fact, Gina kept insisting they should publish a cookbook. They could include fabulous pictures like a glass of sweet iced tea next to a piece of shoofly pie. Just the thought made Agatha's blood sugar rise.

They were going to have a rather full table for dinner with the Wrights, another couple still due to check in, plus the Hochstetlers, Henry and Emma, and possibly Tony. And what about

Joey Troyer? Where was the young man? Who checked into a B&B, then never returned to stay there? She had the check he'd paid with in her desk drawer. Perhaps she should pull it out, look for a contact number, and give him a call.

Then Fonzi brought a mouse into the mud-room, the sink in the kitchen backed up, and all thoughts of her missing guest vanished. The next hour passed consumed by the general bustle of running a B&B.

Fortunately Emma had offered to help with dessert, though Gina protested that guests weren't supposed to cook. "Isn't that why you're on vacation? So you can stop cooking for a few days?"

Emma's only reply was a laugh.

It felt good to have three of them working in the main house. Gina cleaned with her customary vigor. Emma cooked, and Agatha checked in guests and responded to reservation requests. She had an old laptop as well as a landline in her office. Both were quite handy in the day-to-day running of a B&B. Most people stared in amazement when they saw the landline. Some even laughed! Agatha understood cell phones were more convenient, but she had no desire to carry a telephone around in the pocket of her apron.

The B&B didn't have electricity, but its solar power allowed them to charge various things—

like the laptop. Of course, she'd sought and received approval from the bishop for both the laptop and the landline. They were only used for business, and she kept the phone ringer turned off so it wouldn't be a constant interruption. It did, however, ring over to her answering machine.

Since *Englischers* mainly used cell phones, it had become more difficult to actually find answering machines. Sometimes one could be found at a garage sale, which felt like stumbling upon treasure. In every community Agatha had visited, there had been phone shacks that were used by the Plain folk and those phone shacks always included an answering machine.

Being busy on Wednesday morning helped Agatha push the question of Nathan's murder to the back of her mind. It only intruded occasionally—as she paused to write out a list of suspects, when she saw the Hunt Police vehicles pass down the road, and when Henry trudged back from the river. He raised a hand to wave, and she thought the bottom of his pants looked wet. Had he been wading in the river?

There was little traffic on the road as she swept the front porch and tidied the brightly covered cushions on the rocking chairs. She was proud of her little B&B, though she understood pride was a sin. Was it? Did the Bible say that? Or was it only that pride goes before a fall? She'd have to look that up.

She decided to walk toward the road and dead-head the mums in the miniature horse trough she'd positioned next to her sign. The sign read *Plain & Simple B&B*, something Gina teased her about quite regularly. "As if the horse and buggy on the sign don't provide adequate clues that you're Amish."

She liked that about Gina. The woman was always practical and always able to see the humor in things, and she was *straight shootin'* as Texans liked to say. Come to think of it, she'd seen Gina carry a shotgun and the woman probably could shoot straight. Agatha pushed the memory away as Gina joined her in the little garden.

"Becca called from her phone booth. Said you could come by any time this afternoon."

"*Gut.*"

"Snooping around about Nathan?"

"I am not." One look at Gina's face, and Agatha confessed. "A little, maybe. You have to admit it's odd. Why would someone kill Nathan? Why kill him when he's surrounded by his goats? What is the world coming to?"

She waved with the garden tool she was using to prune the chrysanthemums, trying to punctuate her indignation at another murder happening so close to her B&B. But Gina wasn't even paying attention. Instead she grabbed Agatha's arm and nodded toward the road.

"Isn't that your missing guest?"

"Missing guest?"

"Joey Troyer."

A battered green truck drove slowly down the road, accelerating when it passed her property. "Oh, I don't think so."

Was that Joey Troyer driving the vehicle? She hadn't seen the man since he'd checked in the day before. It couldn't be him. Could it?

"I thought he was Amish." Gina craned her neck to better watch the truck disappear. "Was he driving a truck when he checked in yesterday?"

"Huh. I can't remember. I was inside when he knocked on the front door. I didn't actually see . . ."

"If he's Amish, he must have used one of the Uber drivers in town."

"We only have two."

"I'm aware." Gina put her hands on her slim hips.

Agatha knew she ate. So why didn't she gain weight? Agatha was gaining a pound or two a year. She knew it by the way her dresses fit. It seemed to her that Gina was losing weight, and she was finding it. Not a fair exchange at all.

"With only two Uber drivers it shouldn't be hard to figure out who brought Joey Troyer here. Was it Justin? You would have heard Justin's GTO. The engine is loud enough to rattle the glass panes in the windows."

"It wasn't him, I don't think. Maybe Serena?"

"Did she come in to talk? Serena always comes in to talk. I don't know how she makes enough money to keep going, what with all the visiting she does." Gina rolled her eyes, as if the ways of women were beyond her, despite the fact that she was one.

"I guess Joey could have driven a truck."

"Explain that to me." Gina drummed her fingers on the B&B sign. "Buggies, Amish, Plain folk . . . yadda, yadda."

"*Ya*. Sure, but some Amish *youngies* do drive *Englisch* vehicles, especially if they're dragging out the days of their *rumspringa*."

"Like that television show."

"Not like the show." Agatha hadn't actually seen it, but she'd heard details of the plot . . . Gina had described it to her at length. "Non-Amish folk have trouble understanding *rumspringa*."

"Running around time. If you ask me, it's just another way of seeing they get a free pass. We're all too easy on this generation."

Agatha didn't challenge the *we* part of that statement. Gina had no children, though she had several nieces and nephews. And Agatha had never given her own children or grandchildren a free pass. Together the two women walked back toward the front porch.

"I don't begrudge them their running around time." She pulled on her apron, attempting to straighten it. "There will be enough years in the future for them to settle down and follow the rules of their *Ordnung*."

"Humph."

"In my opinion, and believe me there are plenty who disagree on this topic, but in my opinion a few years straddling the *Englisch* and Amish world usually teaches them that they prefer the simple life of the Plain community."

"Doesn't explain why Joey Troyer would check into your B&B driving a truck, then disappear, but cruise by the next day. What could he have been looking for?"

What was he looking for, indeed?

If it was even him.

She didn't know anyone who drove a battered green truck, and theirs was a small town.

Hunt was in point of fact an unincorporated community. Their population had recently topped 1,500, a fact that brought much consternation to the locals. Just the week before she'd heard the butcher declare to a customer in line in front of her, "If we wanted to live in Los Angeles, we'd move there."

Agatha hid her smile by pretending to search for something in her purse. She'd read recently that with real estate prices rising in the cities, people were relocating to the rural areas of the Lone Star state. Still, she didn't think Hunt had to worry about a massive population increase.

But someone might know who the old green

truck belonged to. She could ask around. In Hunt, everyone knew everyone else. They also knew who was just passing through. The fellow driving the old truck hadn't looked like a tourist to her. Tourists usually drove vans or sports cars or motorcycles.

She'd ask around later, while she was out making discreet inquiries about Henry.

She needed to add *old green truck* to her list of clues. She also should call the list something else before she showed it to Tony. Hadn't he warned her against getting involved? She didn't want to find herself caught up in another investigation, but a person couldn't help wondering about such things. The murder had been practically in her back yard. It was natural to keep a list of questions. She wasn't trying to be Miss Marple. She didn't need to hear any more Agatha Christie remarks. Maybe she'd keep the list to herself.

She finished tidying, then she had just enough time to place a few phone calls. She absolutely had to get on the road soon if she hoped to be back to help with setting out an early dinner. Her plan was to harness up Doc, go visit Bishop Jonas, then stop by to see her friend Becca, and finally take a casserole by to Nathan King's family.

Unfortunately the second couple she checked into the B&B wanted to talk. She'd walked them down to their cabin, one of the two new ones she'd added in the last six months. Cabin five was her largest and most expensive. Unlike the smaller cabins, four and five had a separate bedroom and good-sized living room. Cabin four faced the hills, but this cabin—cabin five— looked out over the river.

Valerie and Eric Thompson were from Los Angeles and were looking to relocate to the Texas Hill Country. Agatha tried to imagine the butcher's reaction to that, but only got as far as his look of dismay and the slap of his cleaver against the cutting board.

"What was that?" She tried to sound polite and unhurried.

Eric Thompson was fiddling with his designer sunglasses and staring out toward the water. He was tall and thin and dressed in designer clothes. "We were wondering if you could tell us about the area. We've read the literature, of course."

They had literature?

"We've heard this area is the Napa Valley of the south." Valerie raised her boldly arched eyebrows, waiting for Agatha to confirm or deny that particular rumor.

While Eric Thompson's hair was long and reached his collar, Valerie's was cut quite short. She'd used some sort of gel to cause it to spike all over her head.

"Like Napa? I doubt it, though I've never been."

Valerie flicked her wrist and sighed, as if she'd expected as much.

"It's true that there are quite a few wineries in the area, especially in Fredericksburg, which is to the northeast, about an hour's drive."

"Where the resort is going in? We almost booked there instead of here, but Eric wanted something quaint." Valerie's tone of voice conveyed her opinion on that.

"Your reservation said you were flying into San Antonio," Agatha recalled. "Did you take Interstate 10 or drive the back roads?"

"Ten, if you want to call that an interstate. In California it would hardly be considered a highway. I can only imagine what your back roads are like."

"Smaller." Agatha forced a smile. "Many guests enjoy a drive through the Hill Country. It's beautiful to travel east through Kerrville then south on Highway 173, or you could take the 16 Loop to the west which is also nice though less populated. Either way you end up in Bandera."

"How do you know so much about roads? I thought you people didn't drive."

Agatha ignored the *you people* comment, though it did little to improve her opinion of Valerie Thompson. "It's true that we don't own vehicles, and I only use my mare Doc for short trips, but I try to know enough to inform my guests."

Eric looked as if he were still waiting for something. Agatha tried to remember his original question. *Tell us about the area* . . . "As you probably know, this portion of the state is known as the Hill Country of Texas."

"Capital letters?" Eric asked.

Valerie rolled her eyes and offered, "He's a novelist. Always thinking about words!"

"As a matter of fact, locals do always use capital letters when referring to the Hill Country." She emphasized the last two words, making a little joke, but Valerie and Eric didn't seem to get it.

"Unusual topography," Eric waved his sunglasses toward the hills.

"The hills are limestone. This area of the state separates the coastal plains, which lead to the Gulf of Mexico, from the Edwards Plateau."

"Ah," Eric said.

Valerie plopped into a rocker and pulled her hat down low to block out any sun that might leak onto the covered porch. Everything about her body language indicated she was bored by their conversation.

"Have you been there?" Eric asked. "The Edwards Plateau?"

"I haven't. Texas is big—very big. I've actually only seen a small portion of it."

In truth, she'd been in the state for nearly two years, yet so far managed to see hardly anything outside of the Hill Country. Tony and Gina kept after her to take some time off, but when she did she usually went home to Shipshewana. There were *grandkinner* to cuddle and news to catch up on. She missed her family terribly, but not enough to move back. *Nein*, Texas had somehow claimed her heart in a very short time.

And what wasn't there to love about it?

Eric popped his sunglasses back on. "From a preliminary study of the land for sale, I gather it's quite expensive, though only by Texas standards. By California standards, everything here is a steal."

"Is that so?"

He cast her a side look, without turning his head. It reminded her of a gator.

"I'm surprised *your people* could afford it."

There it was again. Did he even realize he was being patronizing? Agatha felt her hackles rise. Eric Thompson seemed like a rude fellow to her, but then again perhaps he didn't realize that he came across that way.

Agatha took a deep breath, envisioned herself knitting, calmed, and asked, "You're familiar with Amish?"

"A little. I'm working on a book—it's crime fiction, and that subculture was part of my research."

"I see." Though she didn't. "The Amish community here is relatively new. A local heiress,

80

Mrs. Klaassen, had distant family members who were Mennonite. A few years ago, she learned a group of Amish families were considering a move to Texas. Wanting to encourage that, she offered quite a few land tracts at below market value."

"You certainly have a prime spot." This was tossed at her rather like an accusation.

Agatha was deciding she didn't much care for the man in front of her. There was something about him, something more than his curt words and flung glances, that rubbed her the wrong way. Not a charitable admission, but an honest one.

She couldn't resist the urge to defend her ownership of the property. "My brother, Samuel, moved to Texas with the first group. He's the one who started the B&B."

"Huh." Eric looked back at the main house, studied it a moment, then shrugged, as if he couldn't imagine why anyone would want to stay in it, let alone purchase it. "But what do people do here?"

"Hunt is well known for its hiking and fishing, since we're located at a juncture of the North and South Forks of the Guadalupe."

"That's the Guadalupe?" He motioned toward the water. "Not much of a river if you ask me."

Agatha didn't know how to answer that, and she definitely felt as if she'd spent enough time with the Thompsons. "If you need anything else, please let us know."

She turned to go, but Eric wasn't quite finished.

"The land across the river isn't developed."

"The majority of tracts on that side of the river are owned by various non-profit organizations."

Eric scoffed. Agatha wasn't sure she'd ever heard anyone actually scoff before, but that had to be the sound Eric made.

"A waste of prime real estate if you ask me."

"The children don't think so. The nonprofits have cabins and meeting halls and such. Their property is used in the summer as a camp for youth."

"And in the winter?"

"Marriage retreats, corporate meetings, that sort of thing."

"So it's not for sale?"

"*Nein*. It's not."

But as she walked away, Agatha thought she heard Eric Thompson mutter, "Everything's for sale. The only question is the price."

Chapter Six

H^{enry} was standing next to the shuffleboard courts with Emma when an old green pick-up truck passed them. "Looks like an early 1970s Ford."

"My son has been a bad influence on you," Emma declared, shielding her eyes from the sun to get a better look at the truck. "How you both could be interested in *Englisch* trucks—old dilapidated ones at that—is beyond me."

"It's a man thing. Doesn't matter if you're *Englisch* or Amish. Remember the old antique tractors they'd gather together in Shipshewana?"

"I do indeed. Some were steam." Emma shook her head. "Looked dangerous to me."

"Farming has been known to be dangerous, for sure and certain. As for me, I'm glad we still use horses and a plow, but that doesn't stop me from looking when a classic Ford trundles by."

Emma stood on tiptoe to kiss Henry's cheek, sending a flush of pleasure through him.

"Beautiful woman and beautiful weather. *Gotte* is *gut* to this old man."

Emma shook her head in mock exasperation

at the compliment. "Say that after I beat you at another game of shuffleboard."

Which Henry would have liked to have seen. He was moderately good at sending the disc down the court, but Emma? Emma could go professional. Was there a professional shuffleboard team? He didn't know.

Unfortunately their second game didn't happen. Tony pulled into his driveway, poked his head through Agatha's hedge, and said, "Lieutenant Bannister will be here in ten minutes. Care to join us?"

"If you need me . . ."

"We do. Come on in the back door when you're ready." And with that, Tony disappeared back through the hedge.

"Saved by the bell," Emma murmured. "You were worried about losing . . . again."

Her tone was light, but the lines across her forehead indicated she was apprehensive about his interview with the Hunt police.

"I'm sorry. I know it's our vacation."

"No worries, Henry. Go and help as you can."

"What will you do?"

"Are you kidding me? It's sunny and sixty-two degrees."

"I heard there was snow in Monte Vista."

"Indeed, which is why I plan to enjoy today in the Texas Hill Country. I think I'll take my knitting to Agatha's garden and bask in the afternoon sun."

So it was that Henry found himself making his way through the hedge and into Tony's kitchen. He hadn't noticed much about Tony's house when they'd been there earlier with Agatha. Now he took the time to study the room. It was clean and sparse—rather like an Amish kitchen. He supposed that old bachelors and Amish had some things in common. Only Tony wasn't an old bachelor. He was a widower, same as Henry.

Sitting down and accepting the cup of coffee Tony pushed into his hands, Henry realized they were similar in another way. They'd both peered over into the dark side—Tony because it was his job, and Henry because of his gift.

"Did the officers retrieve the bullet from the tree?"

"They did. The Medical Examiner thinks that it certainly could have caused the type of injury Nathan died from, but of course that's a preliminary conclusion."

"How will they know for certain?"

"Blood residue on the bullet. It'll take a few days to get those results back."

They both heard the sound of a car parking out front and the slamming of doors.

"About Bannister," Henry cautioned. "He can be a bit arrogant, and his manners are not the best. Still, he's a good cop. At least I think he is."

"Gotcha."

The doorbell rang, and then Tony was ushering in the lieutenant as well as the female officer who had given them a ride home the day before.

"Henry, this is Lieutenant Bannister and Officer Griffin, who you've already met."

Henry nodded hello to the Lieutenant. The man looked to be in his early fifties, and if Henry wasn't mistaken, had served in the military. His hair was buzzed short, his posture ramrod straight, and his uniform could have passed the toughest of inspections.

Griffin, like the day before, had her hair pulled back with a single elastic band. Henry would guess her to be much younger, maybe even still in her twenties. She somehow managed to display skepticism with her every move. Henry remembered his own self-confidence at that age and almost laughed. When he was in his twenties, he still had no idea how much he didn't know.

The officers passed on coffee and soon all four of them were seated at the table.

Bannister opened with, "Tony has told me about your drawing ability, but I'd like to hear an explanation from you."

So Henry went through the same summary of events he'd told Tony previously—being hit by the baseball as a child, being warned not to use his gift by his parents, and then many years later—involved in Betsy Troyer's investigation.

"In fact, weren't you arrested for Betsy's murder?" Griffin peered at him, as if daring him to talk his way out of that.

"I was. A few days before her disappearance, I had been to speak with Betsy—at the request of her parents. Later, when I was able to reproduce what I'd seen in her room in exact detail, the police thought I must have been involved."

"But you weren't." Tony tapped the envelope of drawings, which was sitting in the middle of the table. "In fact, your drawings pointed the police to Gene Wooten. Subsequently, he was arrested, tried, and found guilty of Betsy's murder."

"Yes, he was."

Those had been terrible days for Henry. He didn't draw again for many years . . . not until a small group had moved with him to begin a community in Monte Vista, Colorado. He'd made sure they all were aware of his gift before they'd agreed to join him, and in the end it had been a good thing that he'd done so. Emma had been among the families that made the move to start the new community.

"I did a little research on savants," Bannister admitted. "Still, I can't say I understand it. What I do know for certain is that it's unusual for a person to be involved in two murder cases, but you've been involved in four—one in Goshen and three in Monte Vista."

Henry shrugged. "Five if we count Nathan's death."

"How do you explain that?" Griffin asked.

"I don't. I can't." Henry had to fight the urge to answer defensively. He certainly hadn't planned to spend his vacation this way, but saying so was stating the obvious and only served to make him look uncomfortable. He'd learned long ago that the less said when the police were questioning you, the better.

"I want you to walk me through the drawings." Bannister reached for the envelope. "The sequence, your location, everything."

So Henry did. He didn't find Lieutenant Bannister to be friendly, but neither was he openly hostile. That changed once they'd finished with the drawings . . .

"Are you familiar with the term serial killers, Mr. Lapp?"

Henry frowned. "I suppose. Fortunately, it's not something that we've dealt with in our Plain community."

"Forensic scholars tell us that there are three categories of serial killers—organized, disorganized and mixed." Bannister's expression was grave, his voice devoid of emotion, almost as if he were reciting facts into an empty void. "The last two often return to the scene of the crime. They worry that they've missed something, or sometimes they're simply fascinated with the investigation. It's often how we're able to catch them, by looking at pictures of the crowds surrounding the victim."

Bannister turned to stare at Henry, his eyes cold and unblinking.

"But there was no crowd." Henry met Bannister's gaze. "There was myself, Tony, Agatha, and my *fraa* Emma."

"Correct. I think we can eliminate Tony as a suspect, and few if any serial killers are women."

"Which leaves me."

"Yes, it leaves you." Bannister's lips pressed into a straight, flat line. He leaned forward a fraction of an inch, and now emotion flashed across his expression—anger, impatience, and disgust. He acted as if he was restraining himself from clamoring over the table and grabbing Henry by the suspenders. "Did you do it? Did you kill Nathan King?"

"I did not." Henry knew that Bannister expected him to expound upon his innocence, but what was the point? The entire conversation was ludicrous, though not—in Henry's experience—unexpected.

Bannister pushed away from the table, stood, and skewered Henry with one final glance. Officer Griffin, who had been silent throughout the exchange, popped up beside him. Bannister warned him to stay in the area, and left.

"That was awkward," Tony noted.

"For Bannister, I suspect, and possibly for you."

"Henry, I know you're innocent. I was with you, remember? Besides, I've dealt with my share of killers—and you're not it."

"Indeed." Henry asked, "So will Bannister use the drawings?"

Tony shrugged. "I hope so. Right now, he's guessing."

"Is that a good or bad thing?"

"According to the novelist Agatha Christie, *unless you're good at guessing, it is not much use being a detective.*"

"So it's part of the process."

"It is."

"In that case, I believe I'll go and join Emma in Agatha's garden. There's some whittling I've been meaning to do."

"Whittling?"

"*Ya.* For sure and certain. I make turkey calls, little toys for the *grandkinner*, that sort of thing."

"Bannister thinks you're a serial killer, and you're going to go and whittle."

"Be like the teakettle; when it's up to its neck in hot water, it sings."

"You're going to sing while you whittle?"

Henry stood and clapped Tony on the shoulder. He seemed to be a good person, and he looked so very worried that Henry wanted to ease the man's concern. Plus there were his obvious feelings for

Agatha to consider. "Perhaps I will, my friend. Perhaps I will."

Agatha decided to direct her mare Doc to Nathan King's first. She'd thought it funny that her *bruder* had named a mare Doc. At first, she hadn't understood the name at all. Then her bishop had shared that Samuel loved the soda pop Dr Pepper, first made in the small Texas town of Dublin.

Riding in the buggy, Doc trotting merrily down the country road, Agatha could almost forget the reason for her visit. The smell of the casserole fresh from the oven filled the buggy, sunshine poured through the window, and the day was warm enough that she barely needed the sweater she wore. How she was learning to love Texas. In Indiana there was already snow on the ground. She couldn't claim to miss shoveling snow or the way the cold temperatures had made her arthritis ache. She certainly understood the reason so many snowbirds chose to winter in the Texas Hill County.

Since Nathan was unmarried, he still lived on his parents' property. Of course she knew Nathan's parents. Their community was small enough that everyone knew everyone else, but she didn't know them well. Titus and Naomi King were a good bit older than she was. In fact, she might have heard someone say that both

Nathan's father and mother had recently turned ninety.

Titus was sitting on the front porch, surrounded by several of the men from their congregation.

"I'm quite sorry for your loss, Titus."

"*Gotte's wille*, Agatha. But thank you for the sentiment."

His eyes were red-rimmed, and his shoulders slumped. Surely all things were God's will, since God was God. He was the creator of the universe. What could pass without His notice? And yet, Agatha understood that knowing someone was in the hand of God and missing them were two very different things.

She squeezed Titus's hand, then made her way into the house. As she walked inside, Eunice Yutzy walked out. Eunice's brother had moved to Hunt with the first group, and she had soon followed. As far as Agatha was aware, the woman had never been married. She was the same size as Agatha, which was to say a little round for her height, with blue eyes that darted about a lot and freckles across the bridge of her nose.

"Real tragedy," she said.

"Indeed."

"You're the one who found him?"

"*Ya*." Agatha thought of explaining that she had been with Tony, Emma, and Henry, but decided she didn't have the time. "I need to get this casserole inside."

"Sure, *ya*." But Agatha had barely stepped toward the door when Eunice grasped her arm. "Be careful, Agatha. Wouldn't want anything to happen to you."

And then, quick as a fox, the woman was gone.

It was an odd comment to make, but then Eunice had always struck Agatha as being a tad off kilter.

Naomi sat at the kitchen table, alone. Her skin was paper thin, her hair pure white, and Naomi's frame seemed to grow a tad smaller each year. She glanced up when Agatha walked into the room, but she didn't speak.

"Naomi, I could have come earlier if I'd known you were alone." Agatha hurried across the kitchen, set the casserole in the oven and turned the temperature to warm. "Gina's cheesy chicken casserole will be perfect for dinner, and I see you have plenty of fresh bread."

Loaves lined the counter—more than Titus and Naomi could eat in a month, but there would be family and the gathering of church members before and after the funeral. In fact, where was everyone?

She poured Naomi a cup of coffee, grabbed a platter of cookies, and sat down at the table, pushing the coffee toward Nathan's mom.

"Why are you alone?"

She didn't think Naomi would answer, but after a moment she looked up and admitted, "I sent them away. Asked if I could just . . . spend a few minutes by myself."

"Would you like me to go?"

"*Nein*. Turns out the pain is the same, whether you're alone or in a gathering."

"Naomi, I'm so sorry."

"Not your fault, Agatha."

"And not what I meant. I meant that I'm sorry this shadow has fallen across your doorstep. Nathan was a *gut* man, and I know that you are going to miss him terribly."

"The circle will be unbroken." She spoke mechanically, as if she were quoting lessons she had yet to grasp.

"Indeed it will be. Until then, we will be beside you, Naomi. We don't even have to talk if you'd rather not. I brought my bag with knitting."

Naomi nodded as if that was preferable, but Agatha had barely begun purling the row of pale blue yarn she was using to make a baby blanket, when Naomi reached across the table and squeezed her hands.

"He was upset the last few days."

"Nathan?"

"One of his goats had died, a doe that he'd had for about two years. Called her Jenny."

"I didn't know female goats were called does."

"*Ya*." Naomi smiled through her tears. "He treated those goats like they were his children—

said they were *Gotte's* creatures placed in his care."

"What happened to Jenny? Had she been sick?"

"Not at all. That was the strange thing. Nathan would lose one now and then—animals die for a variety of reasons, but not because he didn't care for them. He'd even take them into that *Englisch* vet."

Agatha pushed the platter of cookies toward Naomi, who chose one, took a single bite, then set the cookie down.

"Did Nathan take Jenny to the vet?"

"*Nein.* She hadn't been sick. He went out to check on the herd, this was one day last week, and she was just dead."

Agatha thought of the note Henry had included in his drawing. What had it said? *Pay for what* . . . did that have to do with the unexpected death of Jenny? And there was something else she'd seen in the drawing, something that had struck her as odd. Like the whisper of a memory, she couldn't quite remember what it was.

"Nathan thought someone had poisoned her, but he didn't have any proof. Afterwards, after the shock wore off, he wouldn't talk about it. I asked him, but he simply said he'd take care of it. I don't even know what *it* was."

"Did you tell all of this to the police?"

"*Nein.* I don't like . . . involving them."

And yet they were involved, and they would

stay that way until Nathan's murderer was caught.

Agatha waited until a few more women showed up to sit with Naomi, then she slipped back outside. She was walking toward her buggy when Bishop Jonas climbed out of his.

"How are you, Agatha?"

"I'm okay. Naomi isn't doing so well. Come to think of it, neither is Titus. They both look shocked and . . . well, tired."

Jonas nodded, pulling his fingers through his beard. "*Danki* for sharing that. Sometimes people will put on a different expression for their bishop, but for friends they'll show their true feelings. It helps me to know how they're really doing, not how they want me to believe they're doing."

"I understand."

"I imagine when you moved to Texas, you didn't expect to become the next Agatha Christie."

Agatha rolled her eyes. Smiling at the bishop, she confessed, "I've always enjoyed reading her books, so my family teases me with that name constantly."

"If you need anything, let me know. By the way, Nathan's body has been released, and the funeral can be held on Friday."

Agatha hurried on to her buggy, thinking she should skip the visit to her friend's house. She was going ostensibly because Tony had asked her to check on Henry. But did they really doubt that Henry was who he said he was? *Nein*. At least she didn't. Her *to do* list was growing, and she should get on back home.

But she directed Doc toward Becca's. She didn't need to ask about Henry, though she would. And it wasn't so much that she had the time to visit as that she needed to visit. A cup of hot tea on her friend's back porch would surely set the world right, because at the moment everything seemed muddled and confused.

Perhaps Becca could think of a reason that someone would want to poison one of Nathan's goats. Or better yet, maybe she could come up with a list of suspects who might have had a motive to kill Nathan, because Agatha couldn't think of a single name to put on that list.

Chapter Seven

"D o you think the murderer could be someone who was in competition with Nathan?"
Becca's eyebrows were pulled together in a
frown, and it wasn't about the hank of yarn she
was winding into a ball.

Agatha and Becca were sitting on the back
porch, and Becca was using the toes of her right
foot to rock a small cradle where her youngest
grandchild slept. Rose Ann was the cutest thing
Agatha had seen in a very long time. She had an
urge to scoop the child up and cradle her, though
the babe was sleeping peacefully.

Becca, her husband, Saul, and all eight of
their grown children had moved to Texas at the
same time. Whenever Agatha was homesick,
she came to Becca's to be around the children
and grandchildren and chaos. It soothed her soul
until she could make another visit home. She and
Becca were the same age, though her best friend
was two inches taller and twenty pounds lighter.
Agatha tried not to hold that against her.

"What do you mean . . . competition?"

"You know how some people complain that
we're running *Englischers* out of business."

"Who's saying that?" Agatha felt her hackles rise.

Becca simply shook her head and gave her a *you know what I mean* look.

"I suppose Nathan's business was doing well." Agatha had once again pulled out her knitting. It was one of the joys of life to knit on her best friend's back porch and talk through any and every worry on their minds. Nathan's death was certainly on Agatha's mind. "I know last time I spoke with Nathan at church, he said he was booked up six months into the future."

"*Ya*, and those jobs belonged to a landscaping company before Nathan came along with his goats."

"I guess that's true."

"So find out who he put out of business, and you'll find your killer."

"Surely someone wouldn't kill for that . . . for money."

"Humph. Tell that to the person who tried to end your life last year."

Fortunately she couldn't have that conversation because the person was in jail, where he would stay for the rest of his days. But she didn't want to think about that.

Becca's brow smoothed as she moved on to a happier topic. "By the way, has anyone bought the place next door to you?"

"*Ya*. New couple moved in last week."

"What are they like?"

"I've only met them once. We were talking— standing outside at the border of their property and mine, and then both of their cell phones began beeping at the same time and they had to attend to them."

"Typical."

"Certainly they seem nice. They've been busy, obviously. No children that I saw. I think they're . . . what do the *Englisch* call them . . . minials?

"Millennials," Becca said. "I don't even know what that means."

"Tech people. They work from home."

"Ah."

"I guess you've heard that Henry Lapp is staying at my B&B . . ." Agatha finished the row she was knitting, then looked up at her friend. "Henry Lapp who now lives in Monte Vista, who's a bishop, who used to live in Goshen."

Dawning slowly broke across Becca's face. "Bishop Henry Lapp . . . who draws?"

"The same."

"Oh my."

Agatha gave a brief summary of Henry and Emma arriving, their kayak trip across the river, finding Nathan's body, and Henry's drawings. "I'm a little embarrassed, but Tony asked me to see what I could find out about him . . . put it through our Amish grapevine."

"*Gotte* was watching over you when He gave you Tony Vargas as a neighbor."

"Indeed."

"He's a *gut* friend."

"He is."

"And maybe something more?"

Agatha waved the insinuation away.

"Not ready to talk about it, I see. Okay. Well, surely you remember Henry from when we all lived in Indiana."

"That's the problem. I don't. I guess I was pretty busy raising my family then, and I don't remember a thing about a bishop who was an accidental savant."

"Is that what they're calling it?" Becca stood, walked into the kitchen, and returned with a pitcher of iced tea. After refilling their glasses, she sat back down. "It was all very sad—the murder of Betsy, Henry's surprise ability, and then him being arrested."

"Must have been terrible."

"Oh, it was. But the worst part was that some Plain people were willing to entertain notions that Henry had done it. As if they didn't know him better than that. As if he hadn't been their bishop for years—caring for them and praying for them and helping them through all manners of trouble."

Neither woman spoke as they considered such a thing. Finally, Agatha sighed and tucked her knitting into her bag. "A gift like Henry's . . . it's hard to fathom. In my experience, when people don't understand something, it tends to frighten them."

"And when they're frightened, they turn on one another."

"Sometimes." It was a sobering thought that followed Agatha as she made her way back toward the B&B. She hadn't really put to bed any of the worries she'd left with earlier that afternoon.

But she had added several more questions.

And that was as good a place to start as any.

The day was cool, but the wind had calmed.

By late afternoon, her guests had all meandered down to the large living room where she'd set out snacks—freshly baked cookies, oatmeal bars, as well as sliced cheese and crackers. Atop a pinewood table set against the back wall was a tea service complete with a battery powered hot water kettle, various types of herbal tea, and mason jars filled with powdered hot chocolate and various blends of coffee. Brightly colored ceramic coffee drip cones allowed guests to choose their own flavor of coffee. Various blends of freshly ground coffee sat next to locally made coffee mugs.

It was the first time all of her guests had been gathered together. Daniel and Mary Hochstetler were speaking with Henry and Emma. She didn't know their exact ages, but Daniel and Mary certainly seemed older than the other couple by a good ten years. Or perhaps it was simply that they looked dog-tired.

Patsy and Linus Wright were talking to the Thompsons about life in Houston. From the bits and pieces she heard, life in the big city didn't sound like something the Wrights were enjoying. In fact, if she didn't know better they had the look of someone ready to make a move. Is that why they were here? If they were looking for a home, she could put them in touch with a Realtor.

But before she could make her way over to them, Valerie Thompson threw up her hands and stormed out of the room. Eric stood there a moment, rubbing his right eyebrow, then seemed to apologize and take off after his wife.

Agatha hurried over. "Was there a problem?"

"Define problem," Linus said, reaching for another oatmeal bar. "Did you make these? They're fantastic."

"I did, yes. I'd be happy to get you the recipe." She directed the last comment to Patsy, who laughed.

"My wife doesn't cook much," Linus explained.

"I've been known to heat up a meal delivered by one of the local restaurants."

"Yes. She's great with a microwave."

"Linus, on the other hand, loves to spend his time in the kitchen."

Linus patted his stomach. The man wasn't heavy but neither was he thin.

"Was that what you argued with the Thompsons about? Food?"

"Nah. Mrs. Thompson seemed intent on proving that life in Los Angeles was both better and worse than life in Houston." Linus shrugged and took another sip from his coffee mug. "I told her if it was so great, and so terrible, maybe she should go back there."

"Oh my."

"My husband doesn't always play well with others," Patsy explained. If Linus was offended by the comment, he didn't show it. "But seriously, those two are high strung. They don't really seem like the B&B type."

Agatha agreed, but she didn't say so. Instead, she murmured something about checking on dinner and ducked out of the room. She honestly intended to go straight to the kitchen. She didn't. She stepped out the back door and looked toward the Thompson's cabin. Valerie and Eric had stopped on the path and were arguing loudly enough that she could hear their voices, though she couldn't make out what they were saying.

What was that about?

And should she try to intervene?

Before she could make up her mind, Valerie stomped away and Eric meekly followed. Well, couples did argue. Life was full of stress and stopping off at a B&B didn't always cure that.

Agatha moved back inside and set about helping Gina finish up the dinner preparations. By the time she'd served the meal to her guests, grabbed a bite herself, and cleaned up the kitchen, it was a relief to escape to the back porch and enjoy a few moments of quiet.

Apparently she wasn't the only one to have that particular idea. She smiled at the assembled group, quite happy to enjoy the sunset with them.

Not everyone was there, of course.

Joey Troyer was still missing. She supposed she could cancel his reservation and list his room as available for the remainder of the week.

The Hochstetlers had retired to their room, claiming that they'd had a quite busy day and needed to rest. Patsy and Linus were walking by the river. She could just make out their figures as he put his arms around his wife and made as if he was going to throw her in the river. Patsy's laughter drifted back toward the house. They were an interesting couple. That was for certain.

Eric and Valerie hadn't even stayed for dinner, opting instead to drive over to Fredericksburg to eat at the new resort.

"I can't for the life of me think why that Thompson couple didn't stay at the resort." Gina joined Agatha on the back porch. "They turned their nose up at Emma's dessert, and it was the finest pie I've had in some time."

Emma smiled at the compliment. "Your canned peaches made for the perfect blend of sweet and tart."

"They're local," Gina explained. "Fredericksburg peaches. This area used to be filled with peach farms, before the wineries came in, bought everything in sight, and drove up the price of land."

"A story for another day," Agatha quickly intervened. Once Gina started in on the subject of change and prices and the decimation of the Hill Country, it could be a lengthy conversation.

Emma and Henry sat close to one another on the swing.

Tony plopped next to the steps, with his back resting against the porch column. Agatha and Gina settled into rockers.

"How's our murder investigation going?" Gina never was one to mosey around a bush. Her method was more to jump over the bush and yell "AH-HA!" to see what reaction she could get.

Tony told about finding the bullet in the tree, exactly where Henry's drawing had shown it to be. "Bannister sent it off to the lab, but they're quite backed up so it could be weeks before we hear anything."

Henry took up the narrative, describing in detail his interview by Bannister and Griffin.

"They didn't arrest him, so we're taking that as a turn in the right direction." Emma was joking, or at least trying to, but the way she clutched Henry's hand told another story entirely.

Agatha shared what she'd learned from Nathan's mother—which hadn't been much.

"He thought someone poisoned his goat?" Gina rocked her chair more aggressively. "Why would anyone do such a thing? Or was Nathan a little off his . . . rocker?"

"Nathan loved his goats, that's for sure and certain. I mean, not that I talked to him a lot, but the one time we went out . . ." Agatha met Tony's gaze. He looked as if he was trying not to laugh. "Which was over a year ago, Tony Vargas."

"I didn't say a word." He held up his hands in a surrender gesture.

"Why are you laughing?"

"It's just that you never mentioned dating the goat guy."

Agatha rolled her eyes, then she heard the sound of a truck passing out on the road, and that reminded her of her missing guest. She explained about Joey Troyer checking in the day before but never showing back up. Gina chimed in with a brief account of their seeing him earlier that afternoon.

"Or we think we did," Agatha clarified. "It's hard to say, as he turned away while he was driving past, and I couldn't say for sure that he even arrived in an old green truck. I didn't think to look when he checked in."

Henry's head jerked up. "Did you say old green truck? Was it a 1972 Ford?"

"I have no idea. How would I know that?"

"Agatha doesn't know trucks." Gina shook her head as if she'd never understand the ways of her employer. "Now if you asked her what kind of horse was pulling someone's buggy she could describe it down to the right hoof."

"We also saw an old green truck," Emma explained. "Earlier today when we were on the shuffleboard courts."

The group digested that piece of information in silence.

Finally Tony popped up and said, "Back in a second. Don't discuss anything important while I'm gone."

"He thinks he's in charge, because he was a detective." Gina tapped her fingertips on the arm of the rocking chair. "I wish I could think of something important to discuss, but I'm coming up blank."

Tony had gone into Agatha's house. He returned with the pad of paper she kept on the kitchen counter for maintaining a running grocery list. Handing the pad and a pencil to Henry, he shrugged. "Thought maybe your mind picked up on the tag number."

Five minutes later, Henry had finished the quick sketch, and it had been passed around the circle of friends. Agatha's heart quickened as she stared at it. Though only a hastily penciled drawing, it still felt as if the truck could start its motor and drive off the piece of paper. The drawing depicted the truck, a portion of the license plate, and even a crack in the rear windshield. Pulling the sheet closer so that she could better see it under the glow of the solar lights, she ran a finger across a partial bumper sticker that was shaded a darker gray with a star.

"I wonder if this bumper sticker could be a clue."

Tony took the sheet from her. "Dallas Cowboys."

"Who is that?" Agatha asked and was tempted to swat Gina when she started laughing.

"National football team. Their stadium is in the Dallas area."

"But Joey isn't from Dallas. He's from Beeville, and he's Amish. I know he's driving a truck, but sometimes our *youngie* do . . . before they join the church and commit to our ways."

"Could be the sticker was on the truck when he bought it." Henry stared at them thoughtfully. "Of course we have no idea if this Joey Troyer has anything to do with the murder or if the driver of that truck is even him."

Unfortunately, Henry had seen the truck from behind, so he didn't see, unconsciously record, or draw much of the driver, other than it looked like a man with dark hair that reached his collar.

Agatha glanced at Henry, who was watching her. "It's still amazing, to see what you can do."

"*Gotte* is amazing," Henry countered, but he smiled to indicate that he understood what she was saying, what she was struggling with, and perhaps he did. He'd been living with his *gift* for a very long time.

Agatha handed the paper to Tony.

He studied it briefly, then nodded as if he'd expected to see exactly what he was looking at. Folding the sheet once, he stuck it in his pocket. "Good job, Henry. I'll call this in when I get back home. It's only a partial, but we should be able to get something."

Agatha shared that Nathan's funeral would be on Friday.

There didn't seem to be much else to say about the case, so they talked about the weather and upcoming plans for the holidays. Emma yawned and Henry stood, pulling her to her feet. "My *fraa* is falling asleep in your swing. I best get her to bed. We plan to go hiking tomorrow, if the weather allows."

"Partly sunny with highs in the 70s." Gina popped up out of her rocker and began plumping the cushions and generally straightening things that were already straight.

Agatha really couldn't think how she would survive without the woman. If business continued to grow as it had been, she'd need to give her a raise. *Keep your employees well paid and you won't often be in need of help.* She couldn't remember who had said that, but the words rang true.

There was something that people needed more than income, though, and that was appreciation. "*Danki*, Gina." She reached for the woman's arm, and when Gina turned toward her with a look of surprise, Agatha laughed.

"What? I can't thank you for your work?"

"You thank me every week when you hand me a paycheck." She cocked her head to the side, as if she'd better understand Agatha from that viewpoint. "You know I work here because I like it, right?"

"I thought you stuck around because of Agatha's helpful neighbors."

Agatha hadn't realized that Tony had moved closer. She startled at the sound of his voice, then realized she liked him standing so close. She liked the feel of them, together, against whatever lurked out in the darkness. And there was something or someone out there. She could feel it. Her instincts, which she'd learned to trust, told her it was time to be especially careful.

Chapter Eight

The next day dawned sunny and pleasant, just as Gina had predicted. Agatha packed Henry and Emma a picnic lunch, which he was pretty sure wasn't standard fare to be included in the price of a room at a B&B, but she insisted.

"You're helping us crack this case. The least I can do is feed you."

But Henry was determined not to waste the morning worrying over Nathan King's murder. He and Emma walked up and down the riverbank. They paused occasionally to raise his binoculars to the birds and added a painted bunting and a scissor-tailed flycatcher to their life list. They stopped and ate their lunch, enjoying the weather and the view. The water tripped merrily by, its sound a pleasant diversion. Bass slapped the water in search of insects.

Henry breathed in the peace of the Hill Country.

"I'm glad we came." Emma smiled at him as she ran her fingers up and down her *kapp* strings.

"Are you now?"

"I am." When he continued to wait, she added, "In spite of . . . you know."

"Oh, I know."

"Have you ever wondered if that's why *Gotte* gave you this gift, so you can solve murders?"

"Actually, I have thought about that." He motioned toward a bench and they sat.

"And?"

"I have a different theory."

"Hmm. Let's hear it."

"Of course I believe it was part of *Gotte's* plan for my life."

"All things work together for the good . . ."

"Indeed they do." He laced his fingers with hers, looked down at them and thought of how much that sight—two hands clasped together—reminded him of their relationship. They'd truly become one, and that was something he was continually grateful for. He hadn't expected such a blessing at this stage of his life. "I think perhaps I haven't been a *gut* steward of this gift."

Emma tucked her chin, giving him the look.

"Hold on. Hear me out."

"Fine, but I won't tolerate you judging my husband."

He squeezed her hand, then sat back, one arm over the back of the bench, the other fiddling with the binoculars. They'd walked a fair distance down the riverbank, and since the river curved they were now staring back toward Agatha's property.

"When we all moved to Monte Vista, I still hadn't embraced my talent. I was running from it."

"And then Vernon Frey was killed."

"*Ya*, and you suggested that I try to draw what I'd seen at his place. You encouraged me to use my gift."

"It is a gift, Henry. I wish you could see that."

"I'm beginning to, which is the reason that I'm thinking I should stop running from it."

"What do you mean?"

"Even after the murders in Monte Vista, I haven't used this gift to share *Gotte's* love. I haven't used it for anything. The journal you bought me, it's helped me to process things in some way that I don't understand."

"You draw nearly every day now."

"I do, but still I only share it with others when there is an emergency." He nodded toward the opposite bank, toward where they'd found Nathan King's body. "Perhaps I should start using my drawing for better things."

"Such as?"

"Such as this. Look in front of you. Is that not a beautiful scene, a scene filled with the goodness of *Gotte*?"

Another fish broke the water and splashed back down. A turtle on the far side crawled farther out on the log. Sunlight reflected off the water.

"There are many who would find peace in this setting, but not all can come."

"Not everyone has the physical ability to travel," Emma agreed.

"Or the financial means." Henry stood, offered Emma his hand, and they began to retrace their steps, back toward the B&B. "Perhaps it's time for me to start drawing some of *Gotte's* blessings, some of His beauty."

Emma nodded vigorously. "You could make note cards or calendars or even a book of drawings. Those things could be a real blessing to . . ." She stopped abruptly.

"What is it?"

"Up there, where we found Nathan." She reached for the binoculars and focused them across the river. "Look."

Henry peered through the binoculars and pulled them away from his eyes in surprise. "What are they doing up there?"

"I have no idea."

It's no longer a crime scene, but . . ." He couldn't see a kayak tied up at the bank below, so Valerie and Eric must have come at the area from the top. Why had they walked down to the water? Fishing? The Thompsons didn't strike him as the fishing type, and they certainly weren't carrying fishing poles. As he watched, they reversed directions and made their way to the top of the hill.

"*Ya*, but still . . . why would they be there? It's almost as if . . . as if they're searching for something."

Henry peered through the binoculars again, adjusting the focus and finally handing them to

Emma. Without realizing it, they'd both stepped behind a cypress tree. It was doubtful that Valerie and Eric Thompson could see them, but Emma posed a good question. What were they doing at the crime scene? Had they been looking for something?

Henry and Emma continued to follow the path, their attention now completely focused on the couple across the river. They were so absorbed in watching for the Thompsons, they nearly walked into Patsy and Linus Wright. Patsy was snapping photos of the far riverbank, and Linus was standing close to her and pointing first right, then left.

When they saw Henry and Emma, Patsy nodded and held up her camera. "Beautiful area to photograph."

"*Ya.* For sure and certain it is." Henry waggled his binoculars. "We were adding to our life list. Are you two bird watchers?"

"Sure we are." Linus's voice was serious, only the barest hint of a smile tugging at his lips. "Quail, dove, duck."

Patsy continued snapping pictures, though she seemed to be pointing the lens at random spots. "In other words, anything he can stuff a jalapeno into, wrap bacon around, and grill."

"Exactly." Linus cupped a hand at Patsy's elbow, turning her away from them. "Guess we'll see you at dinner."

Henry and Emma continued up the path toward the house.

"They seem like a nice couple."

"Indeed."

"But they weren't looking at birds. Were they?"

"Didn't seem to be."

"Were they watching the Thompsons?"

Henry shrugged. It wasn't his business, and he didn't need any additional complications on this trip.

They let themselves in through the kitchen door, and found Agatha and Tony sitting at the table.

Agatha looked worried, and Tony hadn't touched the cup of coffee sitting in front of him.

"More problems?" Henry asked.

Agatha motioned to the chairs, and both Henry and Emma sat.

"Tony was just telling me that he ran that partial plate you drew."

"The one on the old truck?"

"The same." Agatha nodded to Tony who picked up the story.

"The vehicle is registered to a man named Joey Smith."

"So . . . not Joey Troyer?" Emma looked as confused as Henry felt.

Tony pushed a folded sheet of paper toward them. Henry opened it and studied the driver's license picture. Joey Troyer. A resident of Dallas,

Texas. Age twenty-five. Height five foot, ten inches. Eye color blue.

"So the person driving the old Ford truck isn't your missing guest?"

"That's the problem. This person . . ." Agatha tapped the sheet of paper. "This is the person who checked into my B&B as Joey Troyer."

"Can you think of why he'd used a different name?"

"I can't. There's more though. Why was he pretending to be Amish? Why did he tell me he was from Beeville? And where is he now?" Agatha shook her head, as if she could dispel the worries there. She plastered on a smile, and asked, "How was your morning?"

"*Wunderbaar.*"

"The picnic lunch was lovely, Agatha. *Danki.*" Emma reached across and patted her hand. "We're very much enjoying our stay."

"Except for the murder."

"Speaking of that . . ."

Both Tony and Agatha jerked upright at Henry's words.

"It could be nothing, but we saw the Thompsons across the river, climbing up the bank near the murder site."

"That doesn't make any sense." Agatha pressed her fingertips to her temples. "What were they doing there?"

Henry looked to his wife, who shrugged and

said, "Just stomping around, seemed to be focused on the ground."

"You could see them that well?" Tony asked.

Henry smiled sheepishly, then held up his binoculars. "We were looking at birds, but we . . . ah, stumbled on them. And then as we turned toward home we saw Patsy and Linus. They were on this side of the river, but sort of hidden behind a bush and seemed to be taking pictures of the Thompsons."

"The plot thickens." Agatha pushed up the sleeves of her dress, as if she was ready to get to work. "Tony, you're the detective. I'm depending on you to figure all of this out."

"I'm retired," Tony protested.

"Yes, and you're my fishing guide. So if you want to guide fishermen on our portion of the river, you need to figure out what's happening around here."

Tony tapped his fingers against the table. "I suppose we could go to town. Try to follow up on a few loose ends."

"I was going to garden, but this sounds better. Let me fetch my purse."

Daniel and Mary Hochstetler walked into the kitchen at that point, so all conversation about the investigation stopped. It might have been his imagination, but it seemed to Henry that the two were preoccupied and worried. Perhaps they simply needed a distraction.

"Emma and I were about to try our hand at shuffleboard. Care to join us?"

Mary shrugged, but Daniel nodded. "The sunshine will do us both *gut*."

They all trudged outside. Henry was at the back of the group. When the others had passed out onto the porch, he turned back to Tony and Agatha. "You two be careful. Something tells me the danger hasn't quite passed yet."

Instead of arguing with him, Tony and Agatha exchanged a look, then nodded in agreement.

They took Tony's truck.

"You never ride in my buggy."

"Oh, I don't have anything against outdated modes of transportation."

"You don't?"

"Not at all. But I figured you might be in a hurry to get back to your guests."

"That's the problem with all this . . ." She waved her hand as if to take in the surrounding countryside. "I'm supposed to be living a plain and simple life which, let me tell you, isn't so easy to do when a dead body shows up on or near your property."

"You sound out of sorts."

"I am."

"Hopefully we can find some answers today." He glanced at his watch. "I need to be at the station in twenty minutes. Want to pick up a coffee afterwards?"

She shook her head decisively. "The last thing I need is more caffeine."

"Pie?"

"Now you're just teasing me. You know I rarely turn down pie . . ." She appreciated what he was doing, trying to cheer her up. Why didn't these things bother him? Was it because he'd grown used to murder and investigations and unanswered questions? It was those very unanswered questions that set her teeth on edge. To Agatha they felt like a solid bank of storm clouds, one piling on top of the other until they threatened to block out the sun.

"Pie it is then, and decaf coffee." He gave her that crooked smile she found so endearing. "But first the police station."

He parked a block away and they walked back to the station.

"There were parking spaces in front of the building," she pointed out.

"Yeah, but there's no use poking the bear."

"Who's the bear in this analogy?"

"Lieutenant Bannister."

"And you think he's watching the parking spaces?"

"His office has windows that look out toward the street, out over the parking. I'm not self-absorbed enough to think he's watching for me, but he might happen to glance out and see me, which wouldn't be good. I'm fairly certain that I'm not his favorite person right now."

"Why is that?"

"I honestly have no idea."

They hurried down a concrete walk toward the back of the building, but they didn't go inside. Instead Tony led her around to a small alcove where a woman was sitting on a bench.

"Still take your smoke break at two o'clock sharp, I see."

The woman's face broke into a smile. She jumped up, gave Tony a quick hug and nodded at Agatha. "It's a bad habit but a necessary one if you work for Lieutenant Bannister."

"You were doing this when you worked for me."

"Proving that you two have more in common than one would think."

Tony tried to look offended, but he didn't quite pull it off. "Agatha, this is Julia Perez. She basically runs the police department, though we can't let her know that or she'll demand a raise."

"Fat chance, that."

"Julia, this is my neighbor, Agatha Lapp."

"You own the B&B." It wasn't exactly an accusation, but close enough.

"I do."

Julia took a long pull off the cigarette, studying the two of them. Agatha guessed she was not yet fifty, almost painfully thin, and a life-long smoker, if the lines on her face were any indication. But it was her eyes that were striking. They seemed to take in everything. No doubt she did keep the police department running smoothly. Julia Perez reminded Agatha of Gina. A no-nonsense sort, but also a genuinely good person. She couldn't have explained why she thought that, but Tony seemed to trust the woman and that was good enough recommendation for Agatha.

Julia returned to where she'd been sitting. Tony and Agatha sat on a bench across from her so they could face the woman and talk while keeping their voices low.

"You look as if you want to ask me something." Agatha raised her eyebrows and waited.

Julia nodded once. "That man who did the drawings . . ."

"Henry?"

"Henry *Lapp*." She put a heavy emphasis on the last name and waited.

It took Agatha a few heartbeats to understand what she was waiting for. "Oh, I see. We share the same last name."

"Are you related?"

"*Nein*. Lapp is a very common name among the Amish."

"Huh." Julia tapped ash off the end of her cigarette. "Why the visit, Tony? Haven't seen you since the last murder at Agatha's B&B."

"Hey. That's not fair. Nathan's murder was across from my place."

Julia waved away her objection, keeping her attention on Tony. "What do you want?"

"To know what's going on."

"Go upstairs and ask him."

"We both know how far that would get me." When Julia didn't offer anything else, Tony sat forward, elbows propped on his knees. "I'm not asking for state secrets. Just whatever you'd share at the water fountain."

"They took that out. Someone decided it was bad hygiene. Now there's a vending machine that sells bottles of water for a dollar a pop."

"Julia . . ." Tony spread his hands. "Help a guy out?"

She crushed out her cigarette in a receptacle filled with sand, sighing as she did so. Whether the sigh was for the spent cigarette or due to Tony's request, Agatha couldn't be sure. Standing, Julia said, "I can't tell you anything about Nathan King's murder."

"Because . . ."

"Nothing to tell. As far as I know, Bannister hasn't made any progress on finding the perp."

Tony and Agatha both stood as well. Apparently their impromptu meeting was over before it had properly begun. Tony took off his ball cap and glanced at Agatha as he ran his fingers through his hair. She shrugged. What could they do? They'd tried.

But instead of walking toward the back door of the building, Julia stepped closer to Tony and acted as if she was brushing something off his shoulder. In a voice Agatha could barely make out, though she was standing right next to them, Julia said, "There's something going down on the drug front."

"Like what?"

"Don't know. They're bringing in a canine unit from San Antonio."

"So it's big."

"I guess."

"Who's the informant?"

"Anonymous tip. It must have been a good one, though. Bannister jumped right on it. Watch your back, Tony. When you and Agatha solved that last murder . . ." Here she glanced at Agatha, her expression softening a bit, causing Agatha to realize this woman wasn't as hardened as she wanted to appear. "He thinks you solved that one to make him look bad."

"Not true."

"What's true is relative. Bannister wants a win. He needs a win, and he's not letting anyone get in his way." With that announcement she turned and slipped back into the office.

Ten minutes later they were seated at Sammi's with two cups of decaf and a shared piece of

German chocolate pie between them. Sunlight poured through the plate glass windows. The café was old, but sparkling in its cleanliness. The floor was a checkered black and white, the booth seats covered in red vinyl that was old, broken-in, and soft to the touch.

"Tell me about Julia. She seems like an interesting person, and it's obvious that you think highly of her."

"Julia's a good person. Police departments are filled with good people . . ."

"But?"

Tony forked another piece of the pie, then nudged the plate toward her. "Law enforcement, by its very nature, involves a lot of politics. Every move an officer makes, a department makes, is scrutinized and questioned. Public perception matters. The city budget, and to some extent the police budget, depends on public approval."

"Now you're talking about the current trend to defund police departments."

Tony shrugged. "It's not really anything new. When times are good, citizens are happy for more of their money to go toward making their town safe. But if they think that isn't happening . . ."

"So there are financial pressures as well as logistical ones. I hadn't really thought of that."

"Bannister has a lot of balls to juggle."

"Can you give me an example? And how does

this relate to us?" Agatha sipped her coffee. The pie was heavenly, the coconut perfectly offsetting the smoothness of the chocolate, and she could tell the crust was homemade.

"Well, for a detective or lieutenant or police chief . . . whatever hat you're wearing . . . there's the pressure to make an arrest and make it quickly. Folks watch a lot of TV, and they expect lab results back the next day and criminals behind bars soon after."

"Doesn't always work that way." She was thinking of Russell Dixon. She and Tony never would have caught his killer if they hadn't stumbled upon the motive. It wasn't great detective work so much as luck. They certainly hadn't been trying to make Bannister look bad. "I suppose it's important to at least give the perception that you're making progress."

"Even when there isn't progress to be made." Tony thanked the waitress as she refilled their coffee mugs. He didn't speak again until she'd moved on from their table. "Let's face it—forty percent of murders are never solved."

"That many?"

"More in some areas. Here, we have a pretty good record because murder isn't commonplace. It happens, but people are still surprised by the violence of it."

"And they want to feel safe again."

"They do. That's the department's job—to

give them that assurance as much as to catch criminals. In the best of times, one results in the other."

"But not always."

"No." He put down his fork to indicate he was done.

Tony always left her the last bite. She scooped it up with her fork, popped it into her mouth, and savored it. Chocolate and coconut—they were absolutely perfect together.

As they walked back out toward his truck, she remembered Julia's warning. "What was that about the drug thing? Why would Julia even tell you that?"

"I don't know. I can't see how it's related."

"Yeah. I can't either."

The ride home was largely silent. The day was sunny, there were few cars on the road, and Agatha thought it was terrible to spoil such a wonderful day by thinking about murder. There was nothing she could do about it anyway. She wasn't a sleuth, no matter how much people chose to compare her name with that of Agatha Christie. She was a plain and simple woman running a bed and breakfast. She should stick to what she knew.

Tony parked in his garage, then walked her back over to the B&B.

"You don't have to walk me home, Tony."

"Uh-huh."

"You're not worried—are you? I'm not in any danger."

"Let's just say my spidey sense is on high alert."

Agatha had a deep and abiding respect for intuition, so she reached over and squeezed his arm in appreciation.

They made their way into the kitchen, but heard laughter coming from the living room.

Agatha slipped into her room and tucked away her sweater and purse. Walking back into the kitchen, she stopped by the sink where Gina was washing vegetables. "What'cha making?"

"Stew, with fresh cornbread and a side salad."

"Sounds *wunderbaar*." Agatha tilted her head toward the living room. "Say, that laughter's a nice sound."

Gina closed her eyes in exasperation. "They've been at it for the last half hour. I have no idea what's so funny."

"Huh." Agatha peeked into the sitting area. Daniel and Mary Hochstetler sat on the couch. Henry and Emma were in adjacent chairs. Tony was standing off to one side, studying them.

In the middle of the coffee table was a platter of brownies.

"You made brownies?" Agatha was surprised. Usually she was in charge of desserts and such. Gina preferred cooking the main course.

"I did not. One of your friends dropped them off."

"One of my friends?"

"Found them on the front porch, wrapped in a dish towel."

"No note?"

"Nope."

"Huh."

She walked into the sitting room.

"Agatha, come join us." Daniel was smiling broadly. The expression completely changed his face, erasing the last ten years and apparently a world of worries. Even his wife, Mary, seemed more relaxed.

"Sounds like you're having a fine time."

"Oh *ya*. We were just telling jokes."

"Is that so?" She glanced at Henry, then Emma, then Tony. All three seemed clueless as to what was going on.

"Have you heard the one about the Amish flu?" Daniel asked.

"I haven't."

"First you get a little hoarse, then you get a little buggy."

Agatha suppressed a groan, but Mary seemed to find the joke hilarious. Yikes. Had they found a bottle of the Hill Country wine she kept for special occasions? She snuck a casual look at their mugs, which seemed to be filled with coffee.

Daniel wasn't finished. In fact, Agatha was worried he was just getting started.

"How many Amish people does it take to change a light bulb?"

Mary piped in with perfect timing. "A *what?*" She slapped the couch beside her, laughing and blushing like a schoolgirl.

Tony moved to Agatha's side. He frowned and asked, "Where did the brownies come from?"

"I have no idea."

"How can you have no idea? You're serving them, in your house."

"Gina said someone dropped them off. Why? Is there something wrong with them?"

The expression on Tony's face was an odd mixture of alarm and amusement.

Emma had moved beside Mary. "Would you like to walk out in the garden with me?"

"Why not?" Mary popped up from the couch, but Agatha heard her as she walked out of the room. "Know what vegetable can tie your stomach in knots? String beans!"

Henry sat in Mary's place and tried to interest Daniel in the latest copy of the *Budget*. But Daniel had put his head back and immediately fallen asleep. His snores were actually more comical than his jokes.

"What happened, Henry?" Agatha kept her voice low, not wanting to wake Daniel.

"I don't know. We came down when we heard them laughing. Daniel and Mary were sitting here, enjoying the brownies and telling one another jokes."

"Huh." Agatha didn't know what else to say.

But she immediately forgot about Daniel and Mary Hochstetler and their sudden mirth. Because the sound of a police vehicle's siren chirped twice, followed quickly by the pounding of boots on the front porch and a quick rap on the door.

Chapter Nine

Henry had never seen a canine unit in action, but he had a real appreciation for the intelligence of dogs. His own little beagle, Lexi, was quite smart. She'd actually saved him once, when he was in a very tight situation . . . one much worse than this.

The Hunt Police officer talking to Agatha looked to be the same woman who had given them a ride in her police cruiser. Her name was Gardner, Granger . . . Griffin. That was it. Officer Griffin. Currently Officer Griffin was waving a sheet of paper in front of Agatha and demanding she be allowed to enter. "These men are from the Drug Enforcement Agency, and they have a warrant to search your house. We received an anonymous tip—a very credible anonymous tip."

"I don't understand . . . search for what?"

Tony was looking at the paperwork and frowning. Finally he pulled her and Henry aside and said, "Best just to let them in. I don't know why they think there are drugs here, but I have a bad feeling it has to do with those brownies."

"It would certainly explain the Hochstetlers' change in mood," Henry pointed out. Of course he'd worked with teenagers—yes, even Amish teenagers—enough to know when one was high. He'd simply been a little slow to assign those symptoms to the older couple.

"Brownies? How could they . . . Drugs? I don't have drugs." Then as an afterthought, she asked, "Should I hide the brownies?"

"Wouldn't do any good." Tony nodded toward the canine unit—three German shepherds that were waiting patiently by their handlers' side. All three had black muzzles, intelligent eyes, and coats that were in the main a light tan but gradually blended to a reddish brown.

"If those brownies are laced with marijuana—which I suspect they are—the dogs will figure that out." Tony shook his head and folded back up the warrant, then handed it to her. "There's nothing we can do about it now. Just let them do their job."

Agatha nodded, returned to the front door and opened the screen for the officers, who thanked her and Tony.

There was a moment when Henry thought they were going to have a serious problem. Gina had walked out of the kitchen, taken one look at the dogs and fetched a broom. "Oh no. Those beasts are not coming in this house. I just finished cleaning the floors."

Tony snatched the broom from her hands. "You and I should wait outside."

"Wait? Outside? While these dogs have run of the house?" Gina's voice steadily rose in indignation. "This is a business and a home. You can't expect me to let those dogs . . ."

Henry didn't hear the rest because Tony was literally pulling the woman out onto the front porch. Agatha meekly followed. Henry—realizing Daniel was still asleep on the couch—hurried back into the sitting room.

He sat beside him on the couch, unsure what else to do. Thankfully Emma was still outside with Mary. Perhaps they'd take a long walk and not return until the matter with the police was finished. He could hear the officers upstairs, speaking one-word commands to the dogs, and the soft sound of paws padding from room to room. Leaning forward, he could just see out the front window. Agatha, Tony, and Gina were still on the porch, still arguing over whether the dogs should have access to the house. Peering more closely, he saw that it was mostly Gina arguing. Tony nodded repeatedly in an effort to calm the woman, and Agatha sat staring off across the property.

Agatha was a *gut* woman. Henry and Emma both agreed on that. She was trying to do a *gut* thing here—offering a place of respite for both Plain and *Englisch* folks. Two murders and now planted drugs? Henry couldn't think why such trouble had come across her doorstep. But then he often found himself at a loss for such questions.

As a bishop, he'd tried for years to answer the question of why good people suffered.

He could quote from the book of Job—all that he'd lost and all that he'd regained.

He could trace from Abraham, through Isaac, David, and all the way to the minor prophets. They'd all endured terrible times.

He could even remind those who were questioning of Christ's suffering.

But he'd learned that in the midst of difficult times it rarely helped to point out others' trials. The best he could do was offer a sympathetic ear and offer to pray with and for the person. So that's what he did now. He prayed for Agatha, for the authorities who were seeking to find Nathan King's killer, and even for the killer himself— for surely no one was beyond the reach of God's compassion and mercy.

The DEA officers clomped down the stairs, dogs at their side. One went toward the mud room, another toward the kitchen, and the final officer, a woman with short red hair, came into the living room.

She nodded toward Daniel, who had his head back, his mouth open, and continued to snore quite loudly. "What's wrong with him?"

"Daniel? Just sleeping."

"It's best if you wait outside."

"Yes, well, I would, but Daniel's been having

a bit of a rough visit, and I think it's best not to wake him. So I'll just wait here with him, if that's okay."

The officer shrugged, as if it wasn't worth her time to wake and move the man.

The dog followed her around the perimeter of the room, and then they stopped in the center. The dog—Pete, apparently—sat and placed one paw on the coffee table.

"Good, Pete." The dog sat, wagging its tail and looking up at the red-headed officer, who was now speaking into a shoulder radio microphone. "We have an alert in the living room."

Henry didn't know a lot about drugs. He understood it was a great temptation among the *youngie*. In addition, his community had the occasional adult who struggled with substance abuse. Once it had been a man who was prescribed painkillers. His use of the drugs all too soon resulted in an opioid addiction. Another man in his community had sold fentanyl to members, and a young woman had pedaled methamphetamines.

Englischers thought the Amish were immune to such problems, but of course they weren't. Each time, Henry had worked with the affected, their families, and local authorities to come up with a rehabilitation plan. The intervention that seemed to work best was one-on-one accountability. As long as someone was meeting with the person on a timely, regular basis, the problems could be held at bay.

By and far, the most common drug he'd seen in his community was marijuana. Usually these cases involved *youngies* experimenting, but there were also times that older men and women used it to alleviate some pain—physical or emotional.

So it was that those thoughts, the dog in front of him, and the officer's words all blended in Henry's mind into a dreaded certainty that Tony had been correct.

Daniel's sudden relaxing disposition.

His laughter and jokes.

Mary's light-heartedness.

The plate of brownies.

Someone had served Agatha's guests marijuana-laced brownies. But the bigger question was if and why and how was it related to the murder of Nathan King. Because the odds that those two things were not related were two absurd to calculate.

Agatha was at a complete loss for words as Officer Griffin slipped the cuffs on her wrists and snapped them closed. This simply could not be happening again. Just last year she'd been pulled into the police station for the murder of Russell Dixon, which of course had been ridiculous. She'd also had her wrists duct taped together by Russell Dixon's killer.

Now here she was again—handcuffed. How was it that this kept happening to her? She couldn't make sense of it. Her thoughts kept jumping between that and this, between the past and the present.

She heard Tony trying to reason with Griffin.

She saw the DEA officers standing to the side of her porch with their canine counterparts.

And then Lieutenant Bannister arrived, strutting like a very proud peacock. There was no mistaking the gleam of satisfaction in his eyes.

He accepted the evidence bag holding the brownies from Griffin. "Amish weed. Is that a thing?"

Agatha thought of denying that the brownies were hers, but they had been in her house. Daniel and Mary had obviously eaten some. It certainly explained their behavior.

Oddly enough, it was Gina Phillips who came to her rescue.

"Jimmy Bannister, take those cuffs off Agatha this minute."

"Stay out of this, Gina."

"Stay out of it? You want me to stay out of it? Then you take those cuffs off her right now."

"Why would I do that? I have the evidence right here, not to mention the elderly man in there on the couch and his wife sitting in that lawn chair. They're both so high they could barely give me their names."

"They didn't know what was in the brownies."

"That makes it worse."

"No. It doesn't, because Agatha didn't make those brownies. If you'd just listen!"

"I don't have to listen, Gina. Agatha can attempt to explain herself at the station."

"Do you know my cousin still works at the paper, Jimmy?" Gina pointed at the badge on his shirt. "You may have straightened up your act now, or at least you want everyone to think you have, but some of us remember those charges in high school that were dropped after your daddy wrote a donation check to the police department. You want that story brought back up? Because I have a good memory of the details."

Agatha was now listening aptly, her head swiveling from Gina to Bannister and back again.

Bannister ran a hand over his face, then he stepped closer and lowered his voice. "It's her first offense. More than likely the judge will go easy on her, but I have to process this because we have evidence." He held up the offending bag of brownies and shook it in her face.

"Those are not Agatha's." Gina spoke each word as if it were a complete sentence—as if she needed to speak more slowly so that Bannister could catch up.

"That's what they all say."

"Someone left them on her doorstep, and I'm

the one who found them and brought them in the house."

"Oh, for pity's sake . . ."

"If you want to arrest someone then arrest me."

"Gina . . ."

"I was with Agatha all morning and Tony was with her all afternoon. There's no way she could have made those brownies without us seeing."

"She could have made them yesterday."

"No one baked in my kitchen yesterday, and I will sign a sworn statement to that affect." She took another step forward, literally standing toe to toe with the lieutenant. "Now take off those cuffs."

Bannister was about to refuse.

Agatha could read it in his expression as easily as she could read a recipe.

With a sinking feeling, Agatha knew she would indeed be making a trip to the Hunt Police Department, and this time she wouldn't be sitting outside talking to Julia Perez. She could practically hear the ominous sound of the interview room door closing. A shiver crept down her spine, and she searched for some residual strength, some resolve that could help her through what lay ahead.

But suddenly Patsy Wright was striding across the lawn.

Her husband held back, taking in the scene with solemn eyes.

Patsy walked right up to Bannister, forcing her way between him and Gina, forcing Bannister to back-up. Agatha didn't hear what the woman said to him, but his expression and demeanor suddenly changed.

He looked as if he'd taken a sip of some very sour lemonade, but he put his hands on his hips and jerked his head once toward Griffin, indicating she should take off the cuffs.

As the metal fell away from her wrists, Agatha noticed Fonzi creeping around the corner of the porch, yellow back arched in the shape of a Halloween cut-out, eyes ablaze, and a hiss escaping from his mouth.

Before she could call out, he was dashing across the yard, toward the dogs, who tucked their tails and tripped over one another trying to get back into their handlers' vehicle.

Fonzi must have got in a swipe because there was a whimper from one of the dogs. Officers shouted, the cat dashed back and forth, and the dogs attempted to escape the feline menace intent on attacking. It was all Agatha could do not to drop to the ground and howl in laughter.

The DEA agents managed to load the dogs into the vehicle. They sat there, noses pressed against the windows as Fonzi walked slowly— majestically—across the yard, hopped onto the porch railing and proceeded to methodically clean his coat. Everything about his attitude said that his work here was done!

Ten minutes later, Bannister, Griffin, the dogs, and the DEA agents were gone—taking the brownies with them. Patsy and Linus also vanished.

Gina scrambled an egg and set it on the floor for Fonzi. When Agatha looked at her curiously, she defended herself with, "He earned a special treat."

Agatha somehow helped Gina put together dinner. The stew had been cooking on the back burner of the stove as the drug dogs sniffed their way through the house. All that was left to do was make the cornbread, set out fresh butter, put together a salad, and call everyone to dinner.

Tony didn't join them, explaining before he left that he needed to catch up on a few things at home. Agatha couldn't tell if those things were related to the case or not. He'd asked three times if she was okay until she'd finally shooed him away.

Gina had also left, claiming the excitement had given her a headache. Agatha rather thought she might be going into town to give Bannister another piece of her mind, but Gina assured her that wasn't on the agenda. "I have a yoga class, and after today's excitement, I need it."

Which left Agatha with a small group gathered around the table. Only four of her guests joined her—Henry and Emma, and Daniel and Mary. The Hochstetlers had taken a nap before dinner, and seemed more like their old selves.

Once they'd had their silent prayer and begun eating, Daniel cleared his throat. "I want to apologize for any . . . embarrassment Mary and I might have caused. I have to admit I don't remember much of it, only a sense that perhaps I acted in an improper way."

"Not at all," Agatha assured them. "You told a few jokes, then fell asleep. Nothing to be embarrassed about."

Mary swallowed a spoonful of the stew, then pressed her napkin to her lips. "It's only that the pressure has been so much these last few months . . ."

Her husband reached over and covered her hand with his. Was he comforting her? Or signaling her to be quiet?

They picked at their dinner, then excused themselves.

Agatha watched them slowly walk toward the stairs. "There's something going on with those two. It's worrisome."

Henry had gone out to check on Doc, Agatha's buggy horse. Emma had stayed and was helping with the dishes despite Agatha's insistence that doing dishes wasn't part of the vacation package.

"I think they're carrying a heavy burden," Emma agreed. "I wish there was some way we could help, but until they're ready to talk about it . . ."

"I suppose." Agatha washed another bowl and set it in the rinse water.

"What about the Wrights? Why didn't they join us for dinner?"

"I have no idea." She scrubbed at a serving spoon that had a bit of dried stew clinging to it. "It was so odd, the way they popped up."

"What could she have said to Bannister?"

"I have no idea. Why would she even speak to him?"

"And where did they go afterwards?"

Agatha jerked the hand towel down from its hook. "We need a list. There's so many questions, I can't begin to keep them straight in my head . . . I keep dodging after one, dropping it, and lurching toward another."

"I've always been fond of lists myself," Emma admitted. "Sometimes I add items I've already completed, just for the satisfaction of marking them off."

"Ahh. A kindred spirit."

Which was how Henry happened to find them, twenty minutes later, sitting at the table with a pad of paper and pen resting between them.

"May I?"

"Please do." Agatha smiled at Emma. Agatha was thinking that men might not like making lists, but they usually enjoyed offering suggestions.

Men were problem solvers, in her experience, and Henry did have that special gift of his drawing. Maybe he could illustrate an answer to one of their questions.

"Interesting. This list seems pretty thorough."

Who killed Nathan King?

Why had Joey Troyer/Smith lied and where was he?

Who dropped off marijuana brownies at the B&B?

Who called in the anonymous tip to the DEA?

What had Patsy Wright said to Bannister?

Why were the Thompsons staying at the B&B?

What was really wrong with the Hochstetlers?

"We tried to include everything that's circling in our minds." Agatha was so tired that the tension had seeped out of her as she and Emma had written the list. Now she couldn't stop yawning.

"We could have put sub questions under the main questions," Emma pointed out.

Henry studied his wife, a smile playing on his lips. "Such as?"

"Under that first one—*who killed Nathan*—we could have added the boot print we saw and the corner of the note you drew."

"Plus the tire print, and the bruise on Nathan's neck." Agatha yawned again, attempting to hide it behind her hand.

"Under the Thompsons we could have asked

what they were doing across the river today."

"And why were the Wrights photographing them . . . if that's what they were doing."

Henry sank into a chair beside them. "When you say it like that, I feel as if we haven't made any progress at all."

"Well. We did keep Agatha from being arrested."

Emma smiled broadly, and Agatha realized she'd made a friend for life. Sometimes difficult times did that—drew people closer than they might have become in a year of normal days.

Agatha blinked rapidly, then tried opening her eyes wider.

"Don't fight it." Henry nodded in understanding. "Just go on to bed. Plainly you're worn out."

"I am, and Nathan's funeral is tomorrow." She stood, then pushed in her chair. "Gina made fresh oatmeal raisin cookies. They're on the counter under the dishtowel, and she assured me they are not laced with any illegal substance. Help yourself to an evening snack."

Usually she read her Bible before bed. Sometimes she even knitted a little, but she knew she was too tired for either of those things. She changed into her nightgown, washed her face, and brushed her teeth. With a sigh of satisfaction, she pulled back the covers and crawled into her bed. Then, as she'd done so many times in her life, like she'd done even as a small child, she fell asleep with the words of her prayers on her lips and her heart calling out to God for guidance and help and protection.

Chapter Ten

Agatha awoke the next morning and had to fight the desire to pull the covers over her head. To burrow and forget the challenges of the day was what she wanted most. Given a few minutes she could convince herself that was what she *needed* most. Rather than give in to the urge, she sat up, pulled on her robe and shuffled into the kitchen.

Fonzi had spent the night in the mud room.

When she opened the back door to let him out to take care of his toilet needs, the cat stretched slowly—front paws out in front of him, head down, hind end pointed high in the air. Finally, he padded forward, rubbed against her leg, and walked leisurely out onto the back porch.

It occurred to Agatha that God did a fine job designing a cat. Not just the way they looked—lithe and muscular and fluid—but the way they approached life. Fonzi took each day as it came, rose to the occasion when necessary, and didn't seem to waste time anticipating future trouble or dwelling on that of the past.

She could learn something from the beast.

Once her coffee was made, she poured a cup,

doctored it with a dab of cream, then made her way to the living room. She seemed to have the downstairs area to herself. For once, her guests were sleeping in. The sun wasn't up properly, but the sky had lightened enough for her to gaze out the front window toward the parking area.

There were no cars in her parking area.

Where were her guests?

Henry and Emma had arrived via an Uber driver, as had Daniel and Mary. It was about the only way to get to Hunt, Texas if you didn't drive. Where were the Thompsons? Where were Patsy and Linus Wright? Where was Joey Troyer? Correction . . . Joey Smith.

Surely she was the only B&B owner who had customers check in and then disappear.

She finished her coffee, dressed for Nathan's funeral in her dark grey dress and black apron, and popped the breakfast casserole into the oven.

Gina arrived breathless and full of news. "Apparently after the DEA officers left here, something else happened."

"What else?"

"A big bust." Gina removed her jacket, put it on the peg in the mudroom with her purse, and went to the sink to wash her hands. "Caught some of them too, from what I heard—but not the big guy."

"Caught whom?" Emma asked. "What big guy?"

Gina ignored the first question. "Big guy . . . leader of the operation . . . head honcho."

Henry and Emma walked into the room looking vastly more rested than Agatha felt. Henry said good morning and poured them both a cup of coffee.

Gina checked the casserole in the oven, lowered the temperature to warm, and pulled out a fruit salad she'd put together the day before.

"Gina was just telling me the morning news . . . something about a big bust. But she hasn't explained bust of what?"

"Drug dealers, I guess."

"Here in Hunt?" Agatha now firmly felt as if she wasn't ready for the day. What else was going to happen? A murder. A missing person. Disappearing guests. Now a drug bust! Those were supposed to be big city problems.

"From what I heard, it occurred fairly close to here. Maybe that's why they were snooping around your B&B, Agatha. Maybe their anonymous tip was off a mile or so in the wrong direction."

"Except for the brownies," Emma pointed out.

"True." Agatha closed her eyes and pulled in a deep breath.

She wasn't sure if anonymous tips worked like that. She'd have to ask Tony, only she didn't have time to trot over to his place. She needed to be at the funeral in a couple of hours, and there was work to do here at the B&B before she left.

"Emma and Henry, what are your plans today?"

"Thought we'd take the kayak and go upstream," Henry said.

"Looks like a beautiful day," Emma added. "We need to enjoy the warmth and sunshine while we can. We talked to my son last night, and they had two inches of snow on the ground."

Daniel and Mary shuffled in, looking more like their normal worried selves.

Agatha hopped up to fetch everyone plates. "Did you two have plans today?"

Daniel sighed heavily, as if the idea of filling another day with activities was a bit more than he could manage. "Thought we might try our hand at fishing, if there's no charge to use your fishing poles."

"Of course not. Poles and tackle are in the utility shed past the last cabin. Help yourself. Remember, all the fish are catch and release along this section of the river."

"Oh, I wasn't planning on cleaning fish and cooking them." Daniel stared at the table, dourly contemplating the grain in the wood.

Mary grimaced. "There will be plenty of that type of work once we return home."

The Hochstetlers had definitely settled back into their sour dispositions.

Agatha couldn't sit around and worry about how to cheer them up. She was a B&B owner, not an entertainment director. She grabbed her pad and paper and saw the list she and Emma had made the night before. Pulling the top sheet off, she folded it and placed it in the pocket of her apron. Then she went to her office and spent fifteen minutes jotting down what she could possibly accomplish before going to the funeral.

First and foremost, she needed to prepare for the last two couples who would be arriving for the weekend.

Only when she checked her answering machine, she found that her other two reservations had cancelled. The calls had come in late the previous evening, but she'd been too busy to even notice. One said they'd had a change of heart, whatever that meant. The other said that "apparently now isn't a good time to come."

What were they talking about?

Could they possibly know about Nathan's murder? Or the drug search?

"Probably safer for them if they don't come here," she muttered, not really believing it but feeling better for having voiced the absurd notion.

Agatha mentioned the cancellations to Gina, who didn't look a bit surprised.

"You can probably blame that on social media."

"Social what?"

"You know . . . Facebook, Twitter, Instagram."

"I've heard of those things, but I don't see what they have to do with my B&B guests."

Gina rested her backside against the kitchen sink and crossed her arms. "I didn't want to bring it up."

"Bring what up?"

"The Hunt Breaking News Page."

Agatha waited. Surely her friend and house-keeper would start making sense soon.

"It's like a gossip page, only it's virtual. And . . ." She blew out a sigh. "There's a rumor going around that your B&B might not be the safest place to stay."

"What?" Agatha's stomach began to churn. She pressed a hand against it, as if she could calm her anxieties and fears with the palm of her hand.

"Don't worry about it. No one believes what they read on that page."

"It sounds like the two customers who were supposed to check in this afternoon believed it."

"Perhaps we should rebrand this place as a Murder Mystery Getaway."

"I don't want to be a Murder Mystery Getaway. I'm a plain and simple B&B."

"Tell that to the DEA agents, or Nathan King, or even Russell Dixon."

Agatha blinked three times and waited for Gina to say she was kidding. Apparently she wasn't. "I'm going to make sure Daniel and Mary found the fishing tackle."

"And I'll start cleaning the Thompson and Wright cabins."

Agatha had shared the fact that both were missing when she first awoke.

"Maybe they came back and left early."

Agatha tossed her a you-must-be-kidding look. "Before sunrise?"

Gina shrugged. "If they were out all night, that's all the more reason to tidy their cabins. They'll be ready for a nap when they do make their way back here."

Agatha checked on Daniel and Mary, who had settled for a pleasant morning near the river. Daniel stood in the middle of the stream, water below his knees. Apparently he'd found a pair of waders along with the fishing tackle. He was casting with a fly rod. Mary sat in a chair on the bank, working on some knitting.

"I hope you're enjoying yourself," Agatha called out as she walked toward them.

"We are." Daniel pulled up the tip of the rod and cast the line again, making a nice S shape with the fishing line. He moved down the bank a little, casting as he walked.

Agatha didn't know a lot about fishing, but Tony had taught her a little. She understood that S shape wasn't as easy to make as it looked.

Daniel moved farther away, casting the line toward a small eddy in the water.

"He loves to fish. This is what we envisioned doing in our old age." Mary jerked on the ball of baby blue yarn, her lips settled in a straight line.

"Our plan was to volunteer for a little charity work, relax—fish and knit, maybe even try our hand at shuffleboard."

"That didn't happen?"

Mary glanced at her, then quickly looked back down at her knitting. Instead of answering that question directly, she said, "My *mamm* was one for proverbs."

"Oh, *ya*. Mine too."

"One of her favorites was, *You can tell when you're on the right track. It's usually uphill.*"

Agatha smiled and nodded. "I can remember my *dat* saying that one."

"The problem is that when you're the person trudging uphill, you simply can't tell if it's the right track or not."

Agatha didn't know what to say. She didn't understand what was going on with Daniel and Mary. So she complimented the woman's knitting, then hurried up to the Thompson cabin where Gina was standing on the porch and waving at her.

She'd barely made it up the porch steps when Gina grabbed her arm and pulled her inside, thrusting several sandwich baggies into her hands.

"What's this?"

"That is what I found stuffed between the mattress and box springs."

"Why were you looking there? You were supposed to be making the bed."

"Focus, Agatha. Those baggies are filled with weed."

"What?" Agatha dropped the bags on the floor and took two steps back. The contents had looked like dried herbs to her.

Gina scooped up the baggies. "Each one is labeled with a number—I think it's a location, possibly longitude and latitude."

"You're watching too much television again."

"What else could it mean?"

"I don't know!" Agatha's hands flapped at her side of their own volition. She had to fight the urge to laugh. She was moving quickly from depression to hysterics. "Shouldn't you stop touching them? Your fingerprints are going to be all over the bags."

"Now who's watching too much television?"

"I don't even own one."

"Valerie and Eric Thompson have been up to something from the moment they arrived. It was plain as day they weren't here for the apple crisp."

"I wonder why the DEA agents didn't search the cabins."

"They'd already found what they were looking for on your coffee table." She stepped closer to Agatha and lowered her voice. "That platter of brownies was dropped off on your doorstep, probably by Valerie. She's a crafty one, I'll give her that."

Gina was a no-nonsense woman. She didn't bother with any makeup other than a little blush and a touch of powder. Occasionally she'd pull out a tube of Chap Stick and swipe it across her lips. She was a naturally good-looking woman, but at the moment Agatha noticed the lines of worry between her eyes and around her mouth.

Agatha glanced around, though she knew they were standing in the cabin alone. "You don't think this had anything to do with Nathan's murder do you?"

"They arrived the evening after he died."

"If you killed someone, you wouldn't stick around."

"Normally, you wouldn't." Gina thumbed through the baggies of weed. "Unless that someone had something you needed, like a marijuana crop."

"Nathan King was not growing marijuana." Agatha wished her voice sounded more certain. How well did she really know Nathan? She'd thought him to be a gentle soul, but she hadn't taken the time to learn much about him. He'd been so preoccupied with his goats. She'd assumed they were his entire life. "His business seemed to be doing well."

"Goats aren't cheap."

"I suppose he might have had financial problems of some sort. Still, it's hard to imagine."

"Maybe he'd found the crop and was going

to report the location to the police. Maybe the growers needed to shut him up."

Agatha's legs felt suddenly wobbly.

She sat down in the rocking chair near the window. She could remember picking out that chair, envisioning some nice couple sitting there and enjoying the view. She had not envisioned drug dealers stuffing bags of weed between the mattresses.

"Give those to me." She hopped up and snatched the baggies out of Gina's hands.

"Why? What are you going to do with them?"

"I'll take them to Tony, but first we need to get this cabin back in order." She stomped to the kitchen, found a Tupperware container, and placed the bags inside, sealing the lid tightly. "If Tony's not home, I'll keep these in my office until he gets back. Promise me that if the Thompsons return while I'm at the funeral, you won't confront them about it."

"I wasn't planning on doing any such thing."

"It's best they don't suspect that we know any-thing."

"All good and fine," Gina agreed as they moved to remake the bed. "But when they check their stash and find it missing, they're going to figure something is amiss pretty quickly."

"We'll worry about that when and if it happens. *Sufficient unto the day is the evil thereof.*"

"Amish proverb?"

"Bible. Gospel of Matthew."

They put the cabin back in order, which didn't take long since apparently the Thompsons hadn't spent much time there. Then Agatha hurried over to Tony's with the container of weed, but he wasn't home. He'd left her a note, folded in half and taped to the back door.

Gone to follow up on the boot and tire print. See you after the funeral.

Agatha stared at the note, then put it in her pocket, next to the list she'd made earlier. The words from Matthew that she'd quoted to Gina echoed through her mind.

Sufficient unto the day is the evil thereof.

Each day had trials and challenges. She understood that. She didn't expect perfection when she slipped out of bed in the morning, but this day was developing into something else altogether. She was beginning to suspect that this day might have more than its ordinary amount of trouble. This day was shaping up to be a disaster.

Henry and Emma enjoyed their morning kayaking. After they'd paddled back to Agatha's, he decided to spray off the kayaks. Emma kissed his cheek, then headed back to the main house to make sandwiches. Henry had never heard of a B&B that provided all your meals, but on the other hand there weren't many eating establishments around Agatha's home. He supposed it made sense, but he thought that perhaps she should charge a bit more if she was going to feed people three times a day. After all, it was called a Bed & Breakfast. The title didn't say a word about lunch and dinner.

He had finished with the kayaks and was still thinking of that, of Agatha's generosity, when Valerie Thompson streaked across the yard, barefoot and clutching her designer leather bag. Emma was at that very moment returning with two plates of sandwiches. She gasped, throwing up her hands and tossing the plates in the process. Henry pulled her out of the path of Patsy Wright, who was in hot pursuit of Valerie.

Valerie was plainly winded, and then there was the fact that she'd lost her shoes somewhere.

Patsy, on the other hand, was wearing what looked like athletic shoes, and was apparently in great physical condition. She didn't even seem to be breathing hard. In fact, she looked as if she were rather enjoying the chase.

Valerie was no match for Patsy, who caught her next to the outdoor fire pit, slammed her to the ground, and slapped a pair of handcuffs on her.

"Get off me. Are you crazy? You're ruining my clothes. These are Valentino jeans."

Patsy jerked the woman to her feet. "Those jeans are the least of your problems."

161

"Valentino—twelve hundred dollars, and now I have grass stains on them. You're going to pay for this."

"You have the right to remain silent. Anything you say can and will . . ."

"Eric!" The word came out as a screech.

Henry and Emma both turned to look down the path, and there was Eric. His hands were cuffed behind him as well. Apparently Linus had caught him in the river because he was dripping water and had mud in his hair.

"Tell this woman to un-cuff me right now."

Eric shook his head and let out a heavy sigh, apparently exhausted from his river struggle.

Linus grinned as he passed Henry and Emma. "Morning," he said, winked, then joined his wife.

"She's worried about her jeans."

"Uh-huh. This one tried to swim away from me."

"Guess he didn't realize what an athlete you are."

"Apparently not."

Linus and Patsy marched the Thompsons toward Agatha's. Valerie was still whining about her clothes, and Eric was telling her to shut up. The two were told to sit on the back porch steps. Linus watched over them, arms crossed, feet planted slightly apart. His posture seemed to be daring them to try and run. Patsy stepped aside and pulled out her phone.

"Should we go up there?" Emma asked.

"I suspect it would be better if we stay out of the way."

Agatha had already left for the funeral, but Gina walked outside, took one surprised look at the handcuffed guests and darted back into the house. She returned with a Tupperware container which she handed to Patsy.

"Cookies?" Emma asked.

"Doubtful."

Five minutes later, the Thompsons were loaded in the Wright's vehicle. Linus pulled out of the parking area and turned toward town.

"Where are they going?"

"To the police station, I would imagine."

"Let's go and ask Gina what was in that container."

"And find out who Patsy and Linus Wright actually are."

They never made it to the back porch. They were halfway to the house when Henry heard the unmistakable crack of a gunshot.

Chapter Eleven

Henry veered away from the back porch when he realized the sound of gunfire had originated from Agatha's barn. He sprinted toward the structure. Emma was a few steps behind him and Gina was running to catch up.

All three arrived at the barn door at the same moment, and then Henry heard the clip-clop of a horse and buggy. He sprinted toward the road, but only made it in time to see a buggy with a dent in the back. Had the person been in Agatha's barn? Had they fired a weapon? Why would they do such a thing?

His mind wanted to believe that he'd imagined the sound.

Even if it had been a gunshot, perhaps the person had seen a snake and taken aim at it. But why were they in Agatha's barn? And why had they run away?

The buggy was now out of sight, and Henry understood that staring after it wouldn't produce any answers. He hurried back to the barn. Emma had waited for him at the door, and together they walked into the structure. Henry blinked his eyes, trying to adjust his eyesight to the relative darkness.

"Over here," Gina called out. "Hurry."

The barn wasn't overly large. The main area contained yard equipment, gardening tools and horse supplies. Toward the back were two stalls for horses, though Agatha had only the one mare, Doc—and she was rarely actually in the stall given the area's temperate weather.

Gina's voice came from the farthest stall— the one that should have been empty. She was kneeling by a young man. Henry immediately recognized Joey Troyer . . . or was it Joey Smith . . . from the picture Tony had shown them.

Joey lay on the floor, clutching his side and moaning.

"How bad is it?"

"I have no idea. I've never seen a gunshot wound before."

Henry dropped down beside her, then looked across at Emma and said, "Find us some clean rags. Cotton would be best."

Gina pulled out her phone and dialed 9-1-1, giving the operator their location and the briefest of details. Henry was focused on Joey, but he heard "gunshot" and "hurry" and "I don't know." Pulling the phone away from her ear in exasperation, Gina said, "The dispatcher wants to know if the assailant could still be here."

"I don't think so. I saw someone driving away—in a buggy."

Gina's gaze locked with his. She blinked twice, then relayed the information.

Emma returned with a plastic container of rags that had been laundered and neatly put away. Henry pulled out the largest, folded it twice and then pushed it against the wound.

Joey opened his eyes, gasping in pain.

"Try not to move. We've called the police. They'll be here in a minute with an ambulance."

"Someone shot me."

"Who?" Gina crowded in next to them. "Who shot you?"

"I didn't see who exactly—the person stayed in the shadows." He licked his lips, his gaze darting from Gina to Henry to Emma and back to Henry again. "They said, 'You'll pay for what you've done,' and shot me."

"Man's voice or woman's?" Henry asked.

"I don't know. It was more like a screech." Joey once more sought Henry's gaze, locked his eyes on him.

Henry saw such vulnerability there that he wanted to comfort this man. He wanted to assure him that everything would be fine, and that he could stop running from whatever or whomever was pursuing him.

"Am I dying?"

Henry didn't have a lot of experience with gunshot wounds, but the boy's color looked better and the bleeding seemed to have slowed. He pulled up the cloth as Emma handed him another. "I don't think so. Why were you here . . . in Agatha's barn?"

"I've been sleeping here."

"You paid for a room." Gina stood and stared down at Joey, hands on her hips. "Why would you stay in the barn when you paid for a room?"

"I paid with a check. It's going to bounce. I felt bad about that, so I didn't come back."

"Why did you write a check that you knew was going to bounce?" Emma had wet another of the clean rags with water, wrung it out, and placed it on his head.

"I don't know. I just . . . I needed to talk to Nathan."

Henry, Emma, and Gina exchanged a look.

"You knew Nathan King?"

"Not really. I wanted to, though. That's why I came down here, so I could . . ." But Joey wasn't able to finish the sentence, because suddenly the shriek of a siren filled the air. Faster than a cat could jump off a hay bale, they were surrounded by medical personnel who pushed Henry, Emma, and Gina out of the way.

As the medics tended to Joey, Henry pulled the two women back into the larger room where they wouldn't be heard.

"You saw a buggy?" Gina's hair was short, but

she grabbed a handful of it and squeezed, as if she could clear the thoughts in her head by doing so.

"Heard it and saw it."

"Any idea whose it was?" Emma had crossed her arms, and Henry realized she was shaking.

He stepped closer and slipped an arm around her. "*Nein*. Buggies all look alike. You know how it is. Except . . ."

"Except what?" Gina's look was sharp. "What did you see Henry? Do you need to draw it? Do you need a pen and paper?"

"*Nein*. I remember well enough. There were several dented areas on the back, as if the buggy were old and well-used."

"First the Thompsons' arrest and now this." Gina widened her eyes and shook her head at the same time.

"What did you give to Patsy and Linus? And why were they the ones that were arresting the Thompsons?"

Gina quickly explained about the bags of weed, but before she could answer Emma's second question, the police moved into the room.

Fortunately the officer who had taken the call was Barella. He seemed a tad more pleasant than the woman officer they'd dealt with. "You're the ones who found him?"

All three nodded their head in the affirmative.

"I'll need to take your statements."

They spent the next hour answering his questions, though there wasn't much information they could provide. Henry doubted it was helpful at all, but he knew an investigation could turn on the smallest of details. Still . . . a buggy in an Amish community was rather common. And he didn't know for certain that the buggy had been at Agatha's, only that he saw it hurrying down the road immediately after Joey was shot.

Henry's stomach began to growl, and he realized they'd never eaten their lunch. In fact, where was their lunch?

"I dropped it," Emma admitted. "When Patsy went tearing after Valerie."

The police had roped off the barn area and left, explaining they'd be back within the hour, so Henry and Emma tromped inside and Gina made them sandwiches. Daniel and Mary came in, asking what all the commotion was about, and looking more worried than ever. On hearing the news, Mary declared she needed to lie down, and Daniel followed her out of the room.

"There's something about those two that isn't lining up either." Gina paced back and forth in front of the kitchen table.

After discussing their next move, Gina went into Agatha's office to leave her a note, mumbling that it would "be much easier if certain Amish people would start carrying a cell phone."

Henry and Emma went up to their room to

change out of their clothes, which were still slightly wet from the kayaking and slightly dirty from kneeling in the barn. By the time they'd come downstairs, Gina had called Tony.

"He's going to meet us at the hospital."

They piled into her red jeep. It was a twenty-minute drive to Kerrville, where the nearest hospital was located. They spent the time speculating on why Joey had come to Hunt, who had shot him, and how he'd known Nathan.

They were directed to a waiting room. Fifteen minutes after sitting down, Tony arrived. They huddled in a corner of the room, their voices low and their eyes scanning the area—as if Nathan's killer and the person who shot Joey might jump out from behind the vending machine. Henry realized with a start that they didn't even know if it was one person or two they should be on the alert for. Were Nathan's killer and the person who had shot Joey the same person?

Henry explained how they'd found Joey and went back over what he'd said.

Gina described finding the marijuana in the Thompsons' cabin and then told about giving the bags to Patsy Wright. "She said she was with the DEA. How is that possible? Why are they staying at Agatha's B&B? And if she's with the DEA, who were those people who searched the house yesterday?"

"All good questions." Tony stared at the floor

for a moment, then raised his eyes. "You found marijuana in the Thompsons' room. What did you find in the Wrights' room?"

"I'm offended by that remark. I am not a snoop."

"Of course you aren't. Everyone checks between the mattresses when they make a bed."

"For your information I'm quite thorough when I clean." Gina tried to stop the smile forming on her lips, but she didn't quite manage it. "Okay. I snooped, but I did it for Agatha. As for the Wrights' cabin, it was too clean."

"How can a room be too clean?" Emma asked.

"Trust me when I say we see all kinds of people at the B&B. Everything from the folks who need six pairs of shoes for a three-day trip to the ones who only bring a change of underwear." She gnawed on a thumbnail for a moment. "The thing is that regardless of their wardrobe needs most people do bring stuff."

"Stuff?" Henry locked eyes with Tony, who shrugged.

"Phone cords, laptops, books, crafts, magazines, make-up, favorite pillows . . . stuff." She glanced around the group and grimaced. "Not the Wrights, though. Two changes of clothes, two toothbrushes, and absolutely nothing else."

"Which would make sense if they're DEA agents on an active operation. They wouldn't bring much *stuff*." Tony put air quotes around the last word, then sat back and steepled his fingertips. "I came up empty on the bike tread from Henry's picture . . . it's a pretty standard tire, good for off road or pavement. But the boot print was a little more telling. Johnson Channing recognized the tread and said it's definitely one of his boots."

"He's a boot maker?" Henry asked.

"Yup. Learned the boot making trade from Pablo Jass."

"The Pablo Jass?" Gina let out a whistle when Tony nodded in the affirmative. "There's a long waiting list of folks wanting boots from Pablo. People even sell their place in line."

"Johnson put out his shingle in Hunt fifteen years ago. The interesting thing about the boot print? He changed the type of soles he used after the first couple of years. The soles in the picture Henry drew were the old kind."

Gina crossed her arms, staring across the room at nothing. "So whoever is wearing them probably wasn't Amish. They've only been in the area a few years, so they couldn't have bought them twelve years ago."

"Not exactly true," Henry said. "Amish tend to buy things from second hand shops and garage sales—even boots. So the person could be Amish. They could have bought them used."

Tony was nodding before Henry had finished. "You're right. Knowing who made the boot might not help us find the killer, but once we do find him—the boots will be one more piece of evidence in the case against him."

Bannister walked into the waiting room at the exact moment that the surgeon walked out to update Joey's family. Apparently Bannister informed her there was no family in the area. Needless to say, Henry and his group weren't invited over to listen to the details. It didn't matter. Once the good doctor had finished, Bannister joined them.

"More trouble at Agatha's. Why am I not surprised?"

"How's Joey?" Henry asked.

"He's out of surgery and doing fine. I have an officer in with him now, taking down his statement. Officer Griffin and a forensic team are at Agatha's, processing the crime scene."

They made a tight circle—Lieutenant Bannister, Gina, Tony, Emma and Henry.

It was Tony who asked what was on their minds. "Do you have any idea who did it? In your opinion, is it related to the murder of Nathan? Do you have a working theory?"

Bannister held up his hand to stop the barrage of questions. "Can't say right now. You know that—open case and all. But you can tell Agatha to come out of hiding. We no longer believe she's involved."

It was Emma who jumped to Agatha's defense

before anyone else could. "Agatha isn't hiding. She's at Nathan's funeral."

"Whatever." Bannister actually smiled.

The expression was unusual on him, and Henry had known the man less than a week. Bannister tipped his hat, turned, and began to whistle as he walked out of the waiting room.

"Huh," Gina said.

"He was acting rather . . . odd," Emma noted.

Henry looked at Tony. "What's up with him? Why's he so cheerful?"

"There's only one reason Jimmy Bannister whistles. He's solved a case."

"The murder case?" Gina and Emma asked at once.

"Hard to say. More than likely the drug case. It must have been a big one if they sent two agents down here. I suspect we'll find Valerie and Eric are suppliers for a group of dealers."

"They don't look like drug suppliers."

"That's the problem. Your lower level dealers fit into a typical profile, but the upper level? It can be anyone from a corporate executive to a yuppie couple from California."

"Why would they do it?" Emma shook her head in wonderment. "If they already have a successful life, why would they risk it?"

"Money." Tony shrugged. "Some people just can't get enough. One thing is certain. Based on

Bannister's response, whatever went down at Agatha's today is big."

"How big?" Henry asked.

"Promotion big, would be my guess. Big enough to overshadow Nathan's murder and the attack on Joey . . . or else somehow related to those two events."

It seemed impossible to Henry that Bannister would feel happy about where things stood. Joey Smith was in a hospital bed recovering from his wound, but no one knew who shot him. Nathan King was being buried, and no one had been arrested for his murder. The Thompsons were arrested, but what were they doing in Hunt and was it related to Nathan's murder? It seemed to Henry that very little had been solved, and it felt as if a clock were ticking.

Because he didn't believe for a minute that Valerie or Eric had killed Nathan King. Greedy? Sure. He could picture that, but not murderers. He'd stared into the eyes of a murderer on more than one occasion. He knew what that kind of darkness looked like. The Thompsons were irritating, possibly desperate, and definitely felt they were above the law. But he didn't believe they were killers.

And that meant whoever shot Nathan was still out there.

Chapter Twelve

Agatha had been to many funerals in her life. From a spiritual perspective, Amish tended to see death as a natural event—one that ultimately led to their heavenly home. But the emotional perspective was much the same as that of any group of people. The ones left behind mourned their loss, and so the community mourned with them.

It seemed that most everyone from the Hunt community of Plain folks was at Nathan's funeral.

Looking out across the group, Agatha couldn't tell that a single person was missing. Then she spied Clarence Yutzy standing with his entire family—well, almost his entire family. Eunice was nowhere in sight. Agatha's mind flashed back to her encounter with the woman when she'd gone to see Nathan's mom. What had Eunice said to her?

Be careful, Agatha. Wouldn't want anything to happen to you.

It had struck her as an odd remark then, and now—after all that had happened in the last forty-eight hours—the words took on an ominous feel.

The actual funeral service was held at the King home. It was fortunate that the weather was pleasant, as the crowd was quite large. Apparently some family members had arrived from Ohio, in addition the group seemed to include everyone in their local community as well as a few *Englischers* who had worked with Nathan in a business capacity.

As was their custom at funerals, there was preaching by two of their deacons. Nathan's body had been placed in a pine casket, made by Abraham Miller, who was Becca's brother-in-law. He was a farmer, like most of the Amish men, but he made caskets on the side. He'd once told Agatha that he thought of it as his way of helping those in his community. Agatha knew that people tried to pay him for the work, but Abraham wouldn't accept the money. She'd tried herself when her brother and sister-in-law had died. When Abraham wouldn't take the money, she'd made a contribution to the benevolence fund instead.

Nathan had been dressed in white, as was also their tradition. Agatha thought he looked peaceful, and she was grateful that the mortician who prepared the body had been able to hide the violence of his death. Although it was a solemn time, both the deacons had mentioned Nathan's love for his goats. The fact that they were grazing in the adjacent pasture helped to lighten the mood.

It seemed to Agatha that Nathan had lived a *gut* life, though he had died too soon. And yet as Christians they didn't believe that. They believed in the words of the Psalmist—the very words that Bishop Jonas was reciting at that moment.

All the days ordained for me were written in your book, before one of them came to be.

If that were true, how could it be that his life had been cut short? Who could thwart the plans of God? Yet, he had been shot—killed without regard to the sanctity of life. Surely that had not been God's plan for Nathan before he was even born. Sudden and tragic deaths had always been a mystery to Agatha, one that hadn't become any clearer as she'd aged. Sighing, she realized that she didn't expect to be able to understand all things . . . but it would be helpful to understand the big things.

Still, her faith was stronger than her doubts.

So she sang the hymns.

She murmured *amen* to the sermons.

She spoke words of encouragement to Nathan's parents.

They climbed into their waiting buggies, chalked with a number for ease in finding their own among that great sea of black. The buggy belonging to Nathan's parents was chalked with a number one, since they would be leading the mile long trek to the Amish cemetery—which was actually a corner of Jonas's property.

Once there, they again gathered around the family.

Jonas read from 2 Corinthians, the same verse that Agatha had requested for Samuel and Deborah. Perhaps that memory was what caused tears to blur her sight.

We are confident . . . and would prefer to be away from the body and at home with the Lord.

The pallbearers stepped forward and covered the simple coffin with dirt. Then those assembled flowed past Naomi and Titus, offering words of comfort, promising to pray for them, assuring them that they were not treading through this dark time alone.

Agatha paused in front of the casket, wondering who had chiseled the words on the simple grave marker. For her brother and sister-in-law it had been done by Joseph Schwartz, but he too had passed in the last year. He'd gone on to his reward.

She stood there, tears rolling down her cheeks, and read the words.

Nathan King
12-1-1966
11-3-2020
53 years, 11 months, 2 days

Nathan King was gone, and she realized in that moment that she'd lost more than a fellow church member. She'd lost a friend. The least she could do was help to find his killer.

Agatha found herself squarely in the middle of the long line of buggies that headed back to the King home. The lunch after the funeral was an important part of their traditions. It was a lighter time and tended to provide closure to the events of the day.

Some of the *youngies* had missed the graveyard service in order to set up tables and chairs. Agatha joined the other women who were uncovering dishes—fried chicken, sliced ham, sweet potato and green bean casseroles, plus plenty of fresh bread and an entire table full of desserts.

Agatha was carrying a platter of bread and butter to each table when something streaked across the adjacent pasture. Murmurs rose throughout the crowd, and then some of the *youngies* were standing on the table to see better. Agatha moved back instead, because the house was on a bit of a hill and she could just see over the crowd if she backed all the way up to the house.

A woman was riding a horse, galloping across the field and scattering the goats.

Agatha didn't realize it was Eunice Yutzy until Clarence started running toward her. Bishop Jonas was only a few steps behind him, as were several of the deacons. The real problem came when they accessed the pasture, as they left the gate open.

Eunice cackled with laughter, then took off after the men, spurring her horse first left and then right and twirling what looked like a lasso.

The goats, meanwhile, were desperate to escape the commotion.

They headed straight for the open gate.

Once through, they scattered.

Most headed for the tables loaded with food. A few aimed for the porch, pulling up the bright orange and yellow mums that had been carefully potted.

Agatha remembered suddenly that the males were called bucks or billies. The largest of the bucks climbed on top of one of the tables, sending those sitting there scattering.

A teenaged boy decided to corral the animal, which caused it to grab the end of a tablecloth and pull, then run in the opposite direction. The boy dodged flying dishes as he gave chase.

Several of the baby goats—were they called kids?—stood under a nearby tree, bawling and making quite the ruckus, which caused the does to charge across the crowd in order to reach them.

If only Henry were here to draw this. The thought brought a smile to Agatha's lips. Surely it was a terrible thing to have happen, but the heaviness that had lain across the day lifted. First one, then another of the men began to laugh.

Then the women joined in, and the children were pointing and running after the smallest of the kids.

It took nearly an hour to corral all the animals back into their field. By that time, even Titus and Naomi were smiling. Indeed, Agatha felt as if Nathan must be smiling if it was true that those already ascended could look back down on the happenings of those not yet gone.

The gate was closed on the last of the goats.

Tables were set right.

Dishes were picked up.

Dinner resumed.

Agatha finished her shift at the serving table and went to fetch her purse from inside the house. Her plan was to eat dinner, speak with Titus and Naomi one last time, and then beat a quick retreat. She was ready for the peace and quiet of home. She needed some time knitting, listening to the purr of Fonzi, perhaps sharing a coffee with Tony.

The thought of those things helped her to relax.

So she was brought up short when she came around the corner of the house and heard Clarence scolding Eunice. She didn't mean to eavesdrop, but she stepped backwards and stood there frozen, unsure how to proceed.

"You weren't supposed to come."

"You're not the boss of me, *bruder*."

"And you made a promise, Eunice. Why . . . what were you thinking?"

"Nathan loved those goats. I was simply setting them free."

"They're not your goats to set free." Clarence's voice rose in frustration. "I want you to go home . . . go this very minute. We will speak of this more after I calm down, and after you've had time to think about what you've done."

"Fine. I'll go home. I don't want to be around these people anyway." Eunice's voice, usually whiny and childlike, took on a suddenly menacing tone. "But we won't speak of this again. What I do is none of your concern, and you'd be better off keeping your nose out of my business."

That seemed to be the end of the conversation.

Agatha thought she heard Eunice stomping away.

She peeked around the corner of the house, and what she saw tugged at her already sore heart. Clarence Yutzy stood, his head bowed, his hands on his hips, his shoulders rounded. Obviously he had no idea what to do with his sister. It occurred to Agatha that while Nathan's family would be dealing with their heartache over his death, the man in front of her was carrying a completely different type of burden.

Agatha had no idea how to help him—no words of wisdom, no helpful suggestions. So instead of approaching him, she walked back the way she had come and back through the house.

Her appetite was suddenly gone.

And she didn't really believe she needed to speak with Titus and Naomi today. She'd visit them next week.

For now, she needed to go home.

She needed to rest.

She no longer wanted to think about catching Nathan's murderer. For once, she was happy to leave that to the police.

Chapter Thirteen

Agatha wanted to go to the hospital to visit Joey.

"I'm not sure they'll let you in." Tony had apparently seen that determined look on Agatha's face before, because he added, "But I'm happy to drive you over there if you want to try."

Which was all the encouragement she needed.

Gina agreed to stay late and oversee dinner.

"I'd like to go as well." Henry thumped his cane against the living room floor. He hadn't needed it since the first day they'd arrived, but he did now. He'd learned it was far better to use it and relieve the ache, than to give in to vanity, not use it, and feel worse later.

"Are you sure you're up to it?" Agatha looked at him with genuine concern.

"Because of this?" Henry wagged the cane back and forth and shook his head. "Don't worry about me."

"But you twisted your knee," Emma pointed out. "When you were kneeling beside Joey in the barn. I saw the swelling, Henry, so don't look at me that way."

"*Gotte* has promised to give strength to the weary."

"Another Amish proverb?" Tony asked. "I'm learning you all have a proverb for nearly every situation."

"Indeed we do, but actually I was quoting Isaiah. I'd like to go, if it isn't too much trouble."

"Riding in a car probably isn't going to make it any worse," Emma conceded. "I wish I could go, but I promised to walk with Mary before dinner. I think . . . it seems she wants to share something."

"It's decided then." Henry stroked his beard. "Tony, Agatha, and I will meet with young Joey while you minister to Mary."

They spoke little on the drive over. It seemed that each person was lost in their own thoughts, trying to put together the puzzle of Nathan's death. Henry and Emma would be returning home on Monday, and the sun was setting on a beautiful November Friday afternoon. Henry didn't actually know if he could help solve the murder, but if he could he would have to do so in the next two days.

The afternoon seemed filled and brimming over with color.

The deep blue of the sky.

The brown fields—fallow and ready for winter.

The sparkling river, a light blue that turned darker, then changed to silver as it tumbled south.

The few trees that weren't live oak or cedar sported spots of orange and red and brown leaves.

Henry had never picked up color pencils. He'd never felt the need to use his gift in that way, but now he did. Looking out at a nearly pristine fall afternoon, as the sun slanted toward the western horizon and splashed across the landscape, he wanted to draw the beauty that he saw before him—and he wanted to do so in color.

The clerk at the information desk gave them the number to Joey's room. There wasn't an officer waiting outside. Tony knocked once, waited for Joey to say come in, and all three filed into the room.

He didn't look surprised to see them.

If Henry read his expression right, he actually looked relieved.

"I was hoping you all might come by." His gaze took in the entire group, but settled on Agatha. "I want to apologize to you, Agatha. I lied about who I was, about my ability to pay for my room . . . pretty much about everything."

"No harm done as far as the room, Joey." Agatha smiled brightly at him and motioned toward the visitor's chair. Joey nodded, so she sat and explained, "My inn wasn't full this week, so it isn't as if you took the place of a paying guest. I only wish that you'd told us why you were here and who you were."

Joey nodded as if that made sense, but he didn't

respond to what she'd said. Instead he looked at Henry. "You're the one who saved me."

"My name is Henry Lapp. I was there after you were shot, yes. My *fraa*—that is, my wife, Emma, and Agatha's helper Gina were there as well."

"If you hadn't found me in Agatha's barn, I could have died. The doctor told me that. He said I should thank whoever had provided first aid and slowed the bleeding." He swiped at his eyes, embarrassed by the tears coursing down his cheeks.

He was so young, had so much to learn, and had apparently already struggled mightily in his life. Henry felt great sympathy for him. At least the young man's heart was still tender. Didn't the Apostle Paul encourage them to be kind to one another and tender hearted? There was still hope for young Joey, in spite of the situation he currently found himself in.

"I'm happy that we were all there to help in your time of need."

Joey pulled in a deep breath, then turned his attention to Tony. "I don't know you. Do I?"

"I'm Tony Vargas, Agatha's neighbor."

"I saw you paddle across with Agatha and Henry. When you found the body, your reaction seemed different from theirs. They were surprised and frightened. You were . . . alert."

"Perhaps because I'm a retired detective."

Tony hesitated, then pushed on. "You were in the woods . . . hiding?"

"I guess."

"Do you want to tell us what happened?"

"I already told all that to the police. They took my statement, then left. Do you think they're going to charge me with something?"

"I think if they were, they already would have. Or they'd at least have stationed an officer outside the door to make sure you didn't try to cut and run."

"So I'm free . . . to leave?"

"Well, there is that IV in your arm, and you were shot earlier today. You might want to wait until the doctor releases you."

Joey let out a tremendous sigh, then scrubbed a hand over his face. "You're right. I know you are. Plus, I'm tired of running."

"Why are you even here, Joey?" Agatha tapped her fingertips against her purse. "Why did you use a different name when you checked into my B&B? And what were you doing in the woods?"

Henry thought he might not answer. Joey stared out the window, though the sun had set and darkness was falling. Perhaps it was in that darkness that he saw his answer, because he looked at each of them in turn and said, "I'll answer all your questions, but I think you'll want to pull in some more chairs first."

Tony and Henry snagged two chairs from

adjacent rooms that were empty. It seemed to be a rather slow night at the hospital. No other visitors padded down the hall. A few televisions could be heard playing at a low volume, and the nurses went about their business in their soft-soled shoes.

Once they were all settled, Joey said, "I don't know where to start."

"Start with Nathan. He was a friend of mine." Agatha cocked her head, then added, "I just came from his funeral. How did you know him?"

"I didn't. Not really. I think I need to start before that. I live in Dallas, and I'm not Joey Troyer. My name is Joey Smith."

"We know." Agatha beamed at him. "Tony was able to see a copy of your driver's license."

"How did you do that?"

Tony picked up the narrative. "Henry drew your license plate."

"He drew it?"

"Rather a long story," Henry said.

"I'm afraid you're going to tire so let's skip that part for now." Tony's voice had taken on a business-like tone. "The point is that Agatha and Gina saw your truck, Henry provided the tag number, and I still have friends at the police department."

"Okay. Well, my mom left a long time ago, when I was just a kid. I was living with my dad, but he died in July—July fourth, actually."

Agatha reached forward and patted his hand, and Henry felt even more sympathetic toward the boy. He was, after all, an orphan.

"I'm not telling you that to excuse what I did, but just so you'll understand how I ended up here. After dad passed, all his problems became mine. We had an electric bill going back several months, so they turned the power off. He didn't have any insurance to speak of, but he had the old truck you saw me driving and also a cattle trailer."

"A cattle trailer?" That detail surprised Henry for some reason. "You weren't pulling one when I saw you drive by Agatha's."

"I parked it outside of town, out behind that old service station that's closed down. I hope it's still there."

"How did you end up with a cattle trailer?" Tony wasn't quite interrogating Joey, but Henry could tell that he was mentally taking notes.

"Years ago my grandpa had cattle, and my dad would go out and help him move the cows. Grandpa died, the cattle were sold, but my dad never managed to get around to selling the trailer."

"You wanted to sell your trailer to Nathan?" Agatha looked as perplexed as Henry felt. "How did you even know about him?"

Surely there was someone in a city the size of Dallas who would want to purchase a cattle trailer. Henry and Emma's bus had stopped in Dallas on the way down to Hunt. It was a good five-hour drive from Dallas to the Hill Country.

"See, that's where I thought it was providence or God or something. I don't know. That seems silly now, but one night I came home from my job . . . I was working at the gym near my house. Cleaning floors and stuff like that. Didn't make enough to pay the bills my dad left, but I could eat and pay our rent and that was working okay until the electricity was cut off. Anyway. I came home late one night and there's this news story on the local channel about a guy using goats to clean up the parks."

"It's better than using chemicals." Agatha's expression turned solemn. "At least Nathan thought so."

"Then at the end of the news piece they mention Nathan King cleaning up the banks of the Guadalupe. I see this Amish guy, and I figured maybe he would hire me to move his goats from one place to another. After all . . ."

"You have a cattle trailer." Tony had been watching Joey closely, but it was the first time he'd interrupted him.

"Right. I knew Amish guys didn't use trucks or cars or they could get shot."

"Shot?" Henry shook his head. "You lost me."

"You know. Amish mafia. You guys have a mafia and if someone misbehaves, you . . ."

"*Nein*. We don't." Agatha crossed her arms and looked ready to take on the producers of the once-popular television show. Everyone had heard of it. Even Henry had heard of it, and he knew very little about *Englisch* television.

"Oh."

Joey reached for the cup of water on his tray table and drank it all. Agatha jumped up to refill the cup.

"I guess I shouldn't believe everything I see on TV. My dad used to always tell me that."

"Your dad sounds like a wise man," Henry offered.

"In some ways. Maybe. But there were all those bills . . ."

Tony glanced at the clock on the wall then back at Joey. "So you came down to talk to Nathan?"

"Exactly, but I thought . . . again, I got this from the show which was probably wrong . . . I thought I needed to be Amish. I was pretty sure that he wouldn't even consider my plan unless I showed up . . . you know." He pointed to his badly cut hair. "I cut my hair with a bowl over my head, and then I found the clothes at a Goodwill near me. That was easy enough as you all don't exactly dress in a stylish fashion. No offense."

"None taken," Henry murmured.

Agatha had sat back and was again entranced with Joey's story, as was Henry.

"I booked a room at Agatha's, thinking she could vouch for me."

"I didn't even know you."

"Sure, but you seemed nice, and your website said you welcome all kinds of people—Amish or not. You even have a good Yahoo rating."

Instead of looking pleased, Agatha sighed. "I don't know what that is."

Tony again steered the conversation back on course. "You cut your hair, donned some suspenders, checked in with Agatha under the name Troyer . . ."

"And then you went in search of Nathan," Agatha said.

"Right. To ask him if I could work with him, if I could move his goats with my trailer. I kind of envisioned, like a partnership."

"Nathan had an arrangement with one of the local farmers." Agatha smiled to soften the blow of her words.

"That makes sense. I guess I was hoping I could interest him by doing it for less money. So I parked down the road from where I saw his goats—on the other side of the river—and then I walked back. Only someone beat me there. I don't know who it was. I don't even know if it was a man or woman. Literally, as soon as I rounded the corner I heard the crack of a gun being fired. Believe me, I know what that sounds like. My part of Dallas isn't so good. So I ran, and I hid."

194

"And you saw us paddle across."

"Yeah. I knew when you called 9-1-1 that the police would be there in no time, so I hightailed it out of there."

"Why did you stick around? Why were you sleeping in my barn?"

Joey had been quite forthcoming, in Henry's opinion. He hadn't seemed to hold anything back, but now he stared at the blanket on his bed, rubbing his fingers back and forth over it. When he finally spoke his voice was quieter, almost— almost embarrassed.

"I don't really know. I watched you, how you were with your guests, and I thought that you had a really nice place. I guess maybe I was trying to work up my nerve to see if you needed help around the place." Now he looked up and locked gazes with Agatha. "I'm real good at cleaning things."

"I have Gina for that." Agatha's voice was a whisper.

"Yeah. That makes sense. The thing is that I don't mind doing the gritty work, and honestly the thought of going back to Dallas to that gym that stank of sweat and urine and my apartment that didn't have electricity . . . well, it made me kind of nauseous to even think about it."

Tony leaned forward, elbows braced on knees. In two days, Henry had seen that expression and body language before. It indicated that Tony was ready to drill down to the crux of the matter.

"Why would someone shoot you?"

"I don't know. Honestly, I don't. I didn't see Nathan's killer, but maybe they saw me. That's all I could figure."

"You should have gone to the police," Agatha said.

"Sure. Yeah. I guess you're right." But Joey didn't sound convinced.

"Is there anything else you can tell us, Joey?" Henry tried for his most amiable tone—just two guys talking. "Anything at all about the morning Nathan was shot? No detail is too small."

"Honestly, no. Except, well, this might sound a little crazy. I was walking up right when Nathan was about to be shot. Bad luck on my part. Even worse luck on his part." He shook his head as if his bad timing was due to his own stupidity. "I couldn't see the person he was talking to, but I could see Nathan and he looked . . . well, he looked surprised."

"Surprised?" Agatha, Henry, and Tony said the word at the same time.

"Yeah. Not scared, you know. Just . . . surprised."

A nurse tapped on the door, then stuck his head in the room. "Visiting hours are over. You all are welcome to come back tomorrow."

As they were standing to go, Tony turned back to Joey. "What kind of shoes were you wearing?"

"Today? Boots. They're old but at least they've held together. My tennis shoes fell apart. I tried gluing them but . . ."

"Can I look at your shoes, Joey?" Tony's gaze and his tone were dead serious.

"Sure. I guess. They put all my stuff in that cabinet."

As Tony walked across the room, Henry stepped closer to Agatha. He thought that Joey had been honest with them, but then he'd been tricked into feeling sympathetic for a killer before. He closed his eyes and prayed that this time wasn't like that.

Tony opened the cabinet, picked up the boot, and looked at the sole. Then he pulled out his cell phone and tapped on it until he was looking at a photo he'd taken of the drawing Henry had made.

He replaced the shoe to the cabinet and shut the door. "Okay, Joey. Thank you for talking with us."

Henry and Agatha said a quick goodbye before hurrying to catch up with Tony.

"Was it a match?"

"Did he do it?"

"No. It wasn't a match, and I don't think he did it."

Agatha let out the breath that she'd been holding, and Henry did the same.

"Don't look so relieved." They all stepped onto the elevator, and Tony pushed the button for the ground floor. "If Joey isn't the one who murdered Nathan, then the killer's still out there."

"And feeling cornered," Agatha added.

But Henry wasn't thinking about the killer anymore. He wasn't even thinking that helping in the murder investigation was the reason God had brought him to Agatha's pretty B&B along the Guadalupe River. Or maybe it was that God could have brought him to this place at this time for more than one reason.

As they travelled back to the B&B, Henry's thoughts remained on the lost boy in the hospital bed, struggling to become a man and having no idea how to do that.

Chapter Fourteen

They arrived back at the B&B in time to catch the Wrights leaving.

"Aren't you even going to stay the night?" Agatha wasn't sure why, but people reserving rooms and leaving before they fully used them felt like an insult.

"We'd love to stay, Agatha." Linus was grinning as he nodded toward the kitchen. "I was getting lots of great recipes from Gina, and you know I'm a foodie."

"What's a foodie?"

"Someone who loves food, of course." Gina stood in the doorway between the kitchen and sitting room. "In Linus's case, the term refers to someone who enjoys cooking."

"Guilty."

"I know you aren't going to leave before trying Agatha's apple strudel with a cup of coffee."

Linus looked at Patsy who shrugged.

"Deal."

They all trooped into the kitchen, and five minutes later they were seated around the table with steaming cups of coffee and fresh strudel topped with small scoops of ice cream. Comfort food was just what Agatha needed. She'd been feeling very unsettled since leaving the hospital. She'd made the strudel the week before and frozen it in their gas-powered freezer. Gina had defrosted it, baked it at a nice low setting that didn't dry the pastry out, then broiled it for a moment, causing the icing to brown to a light crisp.

The coffee was decaffeinated, but rich.

The strudel and ice cream were sublime.

She should have felt better, calmer even . . . but she didn't. "How much can you tell us about what happened?"

"Ask away . . ." Patsy motioned with her fork. "If I can't say, I'll let you know."

How was it that the woman always looked flawless? Her hair appeared casually styled, yet perfect. Her make-up, something Agatha had never worn, highlighted her cheekbones and softened her complexion without being over-done.

"You're with DEA." Tony said it as a state-ment.

"Yup. I'm active. Linus is technically retired, but he worked freelance on this one. As you might guess, we met on the job."

"You were here because of an undercover op?"

"Correct."

"How long have you been following the Thompsons?"

"We've been building the case for over a year."

"She's been building the case." Linus looked at his wife fondly. "I've been working on my cooking skills and generally enjoying retirement. Still, when her case took her to the banks of the Guadalupe, I couldn't resist tagging along."

"I told Agatha those Thompson people didn't belong here, especially Valerie." Gina reached for the tub of ice cream and added an additional scoop to her strudel. "It was plain as the Bottega heels on her feet that a B&B wasn't her style."

"Valerie is in fact the one we were after, and she stayed here because she thought Agatha was off the map."

"I'm on the map."

"The resort in Fredericksburg would have been too flashy, or so she reasoned. We're not sure how involved Eric was, but we'll find that out."

"Kind of we already did find out." Linus started to laugh, tossed a look at his wife, and waited for her to nod. When she did, he explained, "Patsy left them in an interview room together and *forgot* . . ."

He used quote marks after the last word.

"*She forgot* to take their cell phones away. Needless to say, Valerie made a call to her top growers, and they have been arrested by the group of DEA agents that were here earlier."

"You can do that?" Henry asked. "I mean . . . it's legal to listen in to their conversation?"

"Oh sure." Patsy scooped out the last bite of strudel and washed it down with the coffee. "There's no expectation of privacy in a police interview room. The evidence is admissible, and it certainly helps our case."

"But they also saw that Eric wasn't quite as complicit as Valerie was. She's bullying him the entire time, and there's even an instance where it's plain he doesn't know what she's talking about."

"Eric is guilty," Patsy reiterated. "But not to the same degree that Valerie is. There's a chance he can cut a deal."

"He seemed like a nice man," Emma murmured.

But Agatha was remembering how obnoxious he'd been the first day she'd checked the couple into the B&B. He might not be as guilty of drug dealing as Valerie was, but she wouldn't exactly describe him as nice—not that a bad attitude warranted a prison term.

Agatha cleared her throat and stared down at the cold strudel sitting in the now soupy ice cream. "What I want to know is, did they kill Nathan? Could they have . . ."

Patsy began shaking her head, but Agatha pushed on with her theory. At this point, it was the only theory they had. She was running out of suspects.

"It's not possible." Patsy crossed her arms on

the table and looked directly at Agatha, as if she needed to make sure Agatha understood what she was saying. "At first we thought so too. A one-hundred-pound drug bust . . ."

"One hundred pounds?" Gina's spoon clattered into her bowl."

"A little over one hundred actually, and we only need ten pounds to make a federal case. The point is that we've put a lot of agents and a lot of hours on this one. When we heard about the killing, we thought they might be connected as well. We checked. The Thompsons were on a plane when Nathan was shot."

"Maybe they hired someone to do it."

"Except we were monitoring all of their com-munication—digital and cellular. We even had an agent on the plane to watch and see if they passed anyone a note. And we've been doing that for weeks. I went back and checked the logs myself. There was nothing about Nathan King in any of it. So unless they're awfully astute, which trust me they're not, then they didn't do it."

"But we saw them over at the murder sight, looking for something." Henry was thinking of the careful way they'd climbed the hill.

"One of their growers had planted a fairly large cannabis field toward the far side of the property, well away from the cabins and such."

"It's SOP for pot growers . . ." Linus interjected.

"Soap?" Agatha felt more confused than ever.

"SOP." Tony smiled at her, looking as if he wanted to laugh but thought better of it. "Standard operating procedure."

"Rather than have their own property, they pay local growers to use someone else's," Patsy continued. "That way if it's found, the owner has to explain why it's there. You'd be surprised the amount of acreage that has absent land owners, or . . . in this case . . . the property is only used certain months of the year. What you saw, Henry, was Valerie and Eric climbing the hill looking for the field of cannabis. Apparently she's not very good at reading a map and headed down instead of up, then retraced her steps."

Henry voiced what Agatha was thinking. "So cannabis was being grown on the same property where Nathan was killed, but those two events weren't related. Seems like a rather large coincidence."

"And yet if we eliminate the impossible . . ."

"Whatever remains must be the truth." Tony tapped the table and nodded in agreement. "Arthur Conan Doyle."

"Valerie was here to check on her growers. Some had been skimming off the top. Some actually did a cut and run. She didn't know about Nathan or his goats. She didn't kill him. It was simply . . . coincidence."

"Then who did kill him?" Emma asked, her voice rising with her frustration. She was usually so quiet that everyone looked at her in surprise. "And who shot Joey? He seemed like such a nice young man. I just don't understand why anyone would do such a thing."

"I'm afraid we can't help you there. Maybe it was simply a homicide, not a murder."

"What's the difference?" Emma asked.

"Murder involves malicious intent." Tony sat back, crossed his arms, and studied the group. "Maybe we've been looking at this all wrong. It's possible that the person who shot Nathan did so by mistake."

"How do you shoot someone by mistake?" Agatha wasn't buying it.

"Perhaps the person was just angry with him and the gun went off accidentally—the person became frightened and ran. Or maybe they were aiming at someone else and hit Nathan by mistake. You'd be surprised at the number of possible scenarios."

It was after the Wrights had said their goodbyes, promising to return the following spring for a real vacation, that Agatha had a moment alone with Tony.

"You don't believe that, do you? That Nathan's murder and Joey's shooting were both simply accidents?"

"It's one possibility." Tony interlaced his fingers with hers as they walked out from under the porch overhang and stared up at the stars.

They stood there a moment, considering that unfathomable majesty.

Finally he looked down at her, put a hand on both of her shoulders, and pulled her close enough to kiss her lightly on the lips. "But no, I don't really think that's what happened."

Agatha's thoughts scattered with the kiss, but she reined them back in. "Then who did it? Who killed Nathan? Who shot Joey?"

"I don't know, Agatha, but it's not our problem. We're going to let Bannister and his officers figure this one out."

Henry slept well that night—for all of three hours. Then he woke with the urgent need to draw. Fortunately, Emma was a deep sleeper. He slipped from the bed, donned his robe, and padded over to the table. Not wanting to turn on the desk lamp, he picked up his drawing tablet and settled in the chair next to the window. The view looked out over the Guadalupe River. He could see very little of the water, only a splash here and there by the light of the late rising moon.

But it soothed him, that sight.

God had made all things. *Through him all things were made.* It had been one of his *dat's* favorite scriptures, and it comforted his heart now, calmed his fears enough for him to draw.

As he did, he remembered that often it was like this. He didn't know what he needed to draw. He simply had an overwhelming urge to do so, as if his subconscious needed to whisper something but hadn't the words—instead he had the pencil and the paper.

He sat there for less than an hour.

Henry couldn't have said whether his drawing was good or bad. He only knew people's reactions to it. And really, their assessment of what he was able to do didn't matter. *Gotte* had given him this gift, as Emma so often reminded him. He was grateful for it.

And perhaps this . . . the sheet in his hand . . . perhaps it would help Agatha in some small way. He closed the journal, placed it on the desk, and slipped back into bed. Within five minutes he was asleep, and this time his dreams lasted until morning.

Daniel and Mary were at the table before Emma and Henry. They had placed their suitcases, two small valises, by the door. Henry squeezed Emma's hand. She'd shared with him before coming down what Mary had said the previous day, and what she hoped might come from that.

As Agatha set breakfast out on the table, she caught everyone up on what they'd learned about Joey Smith.

Mary sat staring at her hands until Agatha joined them at the table and everyone had begun to eat. Then she cleared her throat and looked up. "Agatha, Daniel and I would like to apologize.

We haven't been completely honest with you."

Agatha looked momentarily taken aback, but she managed to regain her composure. "That seems to be going around this week."

"We have no excuse, though." Daniel met Henry's eyes, and Henry nodded once to encourage the man. Confession was good for the soul, and in this case it might be good for their future as well. "We're not dead broke like that young man Joey . . ."

"Near enough," Mary interjected.

"It's true that we've fallen on hard times. We're not from Ohio, as we said. We were, but we moved to Florida hoping to enjoy our retirement years."

"Since we never had any children, it seemed better to sell the farm."

"Only when we arrived in Florida, things weren't quite as they'd seemed. We found the prices there to be quite high . . . astronomical, actually."

"The only way we could make do was to take a loan out on a home and then lease it out to tourists. I guess you could say we're homeless at this point."

Mary and Daniel shared a look, apparently relieved to have their small untruth off their conscious.

"Why would you lie about a thing like that?" Agatha shook her head in disbelief. "It doesn't matter to me where you're from. Though that does explain Mary's reaction to the snake. It didn't make sense that she'd seen a diamondback in Ohio."

"I suppose we still think of Ohio as our home, and Florida . . . I'm not sure it ever will seem that way. Actually we have no idea what to do next, or where to go." Mary reached for her napkin and dabbed at her eyes, then sat up straighter. "We'll think of something, of course we will."

"We're going to have to let the house in Florida go back to the bank, I think."

"Can't you sell it?" Henry asked. He hated to see folks suffer from bad financial decisions. Too often such people took things at face value, or fell for a Ponzi scheme, or simply didn't think a situation through far enough.

"The market has changed again, so it's not worth what we paid for it." Daniel rubbed at the back of his neck. "We're not even sure of our legal options, since we've missed a few payments."

Agatha snapped her fingers. "I know a lawyer here who can help you. Her name's Kiara Bledsoe, and she offered *wunderbaar* assistance to me when I needed it."

"But we can't stay in Hunt. We have nowhere to live. Daniel's too old to work, and we put all of our savings into the Florida place."

Agatha tapped her a finger against her lips.

"Would you be willing to work? I don't mean plowing and such. But would you be willing to be caretakers for a small place?"

"I'd be willing to do anything that took this monkey off my back," Daniel admitted. "I don't mind saying it's robbed me of the ability to enjoy the smallest things."

"I'll put in a call to my bishop then. I think I know just the place. That is, if you're willing to stay in Texas."

"We like it here," Mary admitted. "And your community seems . . . kind."

Which settled the topic. Agatha made a call to Bishop Jonas, explained the situation, and he promised to stop by later in the day.

Henry walked into her office as she was hanging up the phone.

"I only use it for business," she defended herself, looking rather sheepish.

"Ah. Caught by the bishop."

"Indeed."

They both laughed, and then Henry handed her the drawing.

"What is this?"

"The buggy that was pulling away from your barn, after Joey was shot."

She pulled the sheet closer, then reached for her reading glasses that were under a pile of papers on the desk. Perching them on her nose, she studied it again. "We need to get this to Tony."

"I thought so too."

Henry had only caught the last two digits of the buggy's license plate, but perhaps Tony could do something with it. Fortunately, he was home.

"Sure. We can try. Might get a hundred hits, might only get one." His smile was wolfish.

Henry and Agatha waited as he placed a phone call, then turned on his computer and scrolled and tapped, and scrolled some more, before putting in the plate's last two numbers.

The little curser turned into a circle that spun for an inordinate amount of time, and then the computer binged.

"That was quick." Tony leaned forward, Agatha and Henry standing close behind him.

"Three results," Agatha sounded as giddy as Henry felt.

"All here in Hunt county." Tony turned to Henry. "Want to take a ride with me?"

"I'd love nothing more."

"Agatha?"

"*Nein*. I've been running around all week, sticking my nose where it probably doesn't belong. I need to stay home and work today, though I would like to go and see Joey before he's released from the hospital."

Henry and Tony looked at her in surprise.

"It's just that I could use some help around the place. The Blodgett boy has gone off to college, so I'll need someone to care for the horse."

"Joey's from Dallas," Tony pointed out. "I don't think he has experience with horses."

"But he can learn."

Henry nodded in approval. "You have a *gut* heart, Agatha." Then he hurried back to the B&B to tell Emma where he was going. Perhaps they could bring this case to a close before they left after all.

Chapter Fifteen

Tony snagged Agatha's hand as she started back toward her place.

"You're going to stay home and clean?"

"*Ya.* I've been neglecting the place."

"Doesn't sound like you at all."

"What's that supposed to mean?"

"You enjoy putting your nose where it doesn't belong."

"I'm not sure I'd go so far as to say that."

"You never give up on a mystery."

She sighed, crossed her arms, then admitted, "I'm stuck. I can't think of a single lead."

"No leads, huh?" He tucked a stray hair into her *kapp.* "So you're not giving up, you're just . . ."

"Pausing. I'm pausing. Even if you do find the buggy that has those letters Henry drew, I don't think you're going to find the person who shot Joey sitting in it. Most likely the person borrowed the buggy from someone else. Happens all the time. Sort of like leaving the keys in your truck in case someone needs it."

"I would never do that."

"But you've loaned it to someone from time to time."

He nodded in agreement. She knew he'd done that very thing just the week before.

"All right. Just promise me you'll stay out of trouble."

"I'm offended by that remark, Tony Vargas."

"Oh, are you?"

"*Ya*, but it's also kind of sweet." She brushed imaginary lint off his shoulder. "Thank you for worrying about me."

And she did have every intention of staying home and cleaning and baking. The only guests she had were Henry and Emma. Supper would be simple enough. Maybe they could even play some Dutch Blitz afterwards.

She'd given Gina the day off. The woman had worked more than her allotted hours already that week. Emma was in the kitchen, helping her cut biscuit dough into dumplings when there was a thud on the front porch.

"Uh-oh."

They ran out together, only to find a rock, wrapped in newspaper on the front porch.

"Lucky it didn't hit a window."

Carefully pulling the paper off the rock, Agatha was surprised to find nothing else wrapped around it.

"Turn the paper over," Emma said.

And there was the note, written in black permanent marker over the newsprint.

You shouldn't stick your nose where it doesn't belong. If you don't want someone else to get kilt, meet me in one hour.

There was a crude map drawn below the words. "Do you know where that is?" Emma asked.

"I think so."

"Are you going to go?"

"*Ya*. I don't want anyone else to get *kilt* . . ." She rolled her eyes, though some instinct told her this might be a quite serious matter.

"I'm going with you then."

Agatha looked up, studied Emma for a moment, then nodded.

They tried to call Tony, but his phone must have been out of service. It wouldn't even go through to voice mail, which was odd, but then cell service was notoriously bad in their area. Or so people said. Agatha wouldn't know.

Then she called Gina and explained the situation. She held the phone's receiver away from her ear and grimaced at Emma. *She wants to go,* she mouthed, before pulling the receiver closer and addressing Gina. "You can't go with us. Someone needs to tell Tony and Henry when they return. Or keep trying to call him. I couldn't get any answer at all. Emma has drawn out a copy of the note and map. We'll leave it here on the table."

She hung up quickly before Gina could talk her out of it.

"I suppose she wasn't happy."

"Not at all."

"She's a *gut* friend."

"That she is." They were nearly out the door when Agatha turned to Emma and said, "Could you go and fetch Henry's drawing journal?"

"*Ya*. Sure."

Ten minutes later they had Doc hitched to the buggy and had hit the road. Agatha glanced at her watch. The note had said one hour, and they'd already spent twenty-five minutes just getting out of the house.

Emma drove the buggy while Agatha paged through Henry's drawings. "Something has been driving me crazy. Something I saw in one of these drawings . . ."

"Do I turn here?"

"*Nein*. It's another half a mile down the road."

"Are you sure we should be doing this?"

"I am not, but on the other hand what else could we do?"

"True enough."

Agatha stopped pawing through the drawings and looked at Emma. "I'm sorry to drag you into this."

"There was no dragging involved." She smiled, and though it was unwarranted considering where they were headed, it was also genuine.

Agatha liked Emma and hoped they would

216

remain life-long friends. One could never have too many friends.

"My life was rather quiet before I became involved with Henry."

"Was it now?"

"I knew what I was getting into . . . eyes wide open and all that. I didn't know what being a bishop's wife would entail. That kept me awake some nights . . . but this part? Dealing with his gift? I rather feel like it's what *Gotte* intended me to do. Does that make sense?"

Agatha thought of Tony and how smoothly they worked together as a team. Tony, who had been so sad and despondent over the death of his wife. Tony, who had saved her on more than one occasion.

"It does make sense." She glanced back down at the paper in her hands. "That's it!"

Emma jumped and looked at her in surprise.

"Here. Turn here. Then pull over. I want you to look at this." The day had turned cold and the wind had picked up. It was still Texas weather—no snow in the forecast, but the north wind had a bite to it. Agatha rather wished she was home, sitting in her rocker, reading a good book.

That wasn't true.

She was glad she was here, with Emma, and hopefully about to put the question of Nathan's killer to rest.

"We noticed something around the goats' necks."

"I remember that. It didn't make sense though. It's not as if you'd put a halter on a goat."

"But I think someone did." Agatha tapped the drawing. "I think those are rope fibers in the goat's hair."

"Okay. Maybe. But it still doesn't make any sense."

"And then there's the bruising around Nathan's neck."

Emma touched the drawing. "If someone got close enough to choke him, why did they step back and shoot him?"

"Also, we have this bit of tire track . . ."

"Only Tony thinks it belongs to a mountain bike."

"I think so too. And don't forget the piece of paper." She shuffled through the pages again. "Here. This was not written in Nathan's hand-writing. I'm sure of it. Last night I pulled out a note he'd written me. I don't even know why I kept the thing. It wasn't personal at all, just a note telling me he'd enjoyed our date. Anyway, it's not the same handwriting. I'm sure of it."

"Someone was threatening him."

"Reminding him that he was going to *pay* . . . but for what?"

"And what does it have to do with the person who threw the rock onto your porch? Do you think the two notes are related somehow?"

"That's what my mind was trying to remember."

She traced the letters on Henry's drawing. "Look at the way the person makes their letter y, look at the loopy tail."

"Huh."

Agatha pulled out the note they'd found on her front porch only an hour before. The y's were an identical match. "The same person who left this note to me, also sent a note to Nathan—a note he had in his pocket when he was murdered."

"So both are from the killer."

"Maybe." Agatha reached for Emma's hand. "Do you still want to do this? Because I wouldn't blame you one tiny bit if you—"

She never finished the sentence. Emma squeezed her hand, picked up the reins and called out to Doc.

Ten minutes later they were pulling into a remote farm. The fields looked as if they hadn't been planted in some time. The house's roof had long ago caved in, and the barn was leaning slightly.

"There. A bicycle."

It had been left near the corral to the east of the barn.

"And a buggy—an old dented one, near the door of the barn." Agatha slipped the tablet under the seat.

"Should we wait?" Emma glanced back the way they had come. "Tony and Henry can't be far behind."

"The note said one hour. I think . . . I think it's been close to that."

"Okay. Fine. Then we go in together."

"Let's leave Doc back here. In case there's any shooting." Even as the words came out of Agatha's mouth she had to suppress the urge to laugh. Surely she was being dramatic. Surely someone wasn't lying in wait, pistol drawn, ready to put a bullet through their hearts.

Nein.

She wasn't certain about much in this life, but she was certain that she wasn't going to die today from a gunshot.

You would know.

Wouldn't you know?

You'd have some sense of impending doom. All she'd woken with was a hankering to cook a cobbler and a pressing desire to finish the baby blanket she was knitting.

They walked toward the corral, holding onto their *kapp* strings, the north wind tugging at their dresses.

Agatha bent over the bicycle tire, comparing the treads to what she'd seen in Henry's picture. If her memory was clear, and she knew it was, they were a perfect match.

She stood to call out to Emma, who was peering into the corral, when she heard a swish and then felt something tug her shoulders. She looked down to find a rope wrapped around her upper body, and then from behind she heard a satisfied laugh.

"Easier to rope than a goat, that's for certain."

Emma lurched toward her friend.

"Don't do it. I'll pull her off her feet and across that pasture." Quick as a cat sprinting toward fresh milk, the other end of the rope was wrapped around a saddle which sat atop a pretty black gelding. "Beauty here likes to run. All it will take is one slap from me. So you best stay where you are, Emma Lapp."

Agatha met Emma's eyes. Neither said a word.

"What do you say we all go into the barn?"

Which was a terrible idea in Agatha's opinion. The barn looked as dangerous as the person standing in front of them.

"At least it'll be out of the wind," Emma muttered.

She went first. As she passed Agatha, she pretended to stumble into her and whispered, "Henry and Tony will be here soon." Then she marched forward, head held high and back straight. Agatha followed, and Nathan's killer brought up the rear. The barn would have been dark, but there were holes in the roof that allowed some of the scant afternoon light to reach them.

Nathan's killer stopped to free the other end of the rope from the gelding, then slapped its rear, sending the horse into a gallop across the pasture.

Agatha could have been dragged to her death!

221

She would have at least suffered a concussion and some good bruises. It was a sobering thought.

"Agatha, I want you to knock that crate over and sit down on it. That's good. Now Emma, fetch another and put it beside your friend. Not facing, back to back."

Again the cackle, but this time it sent shivers up Agatha's spine. It was the laugh of insanity, of a person beyond reason.

Once they were both seated, Nathan's killer fetched another rope off the wall, slipped it over Emma's shoulders, and then walked around the two women, binding them together.

"This is my best calf rope. Four-strand texturized poly-blend. It's guaranteed to hold up in all weather conditions. Reliable. That's important. Don't you think? Reliability? You ought to feel honored."

"Well, we don't." Agatha's temper was rising. "This is ridiculous. Let us go this minute or . . ."

"Or what? You going to call the police? Oops. No cell phone so you can't. You can't even call that boyfriend *dee-tective* of yours. And by the time Henry gets here to draw what he sees, I'll be long gone."

Lickety-split, the killer had secured a tight knot in the rope. Agatha's left shoulder was beginning to hurt already, and the throbbing pain wasn't helping her temper one bit.

"Why did you do it? Why did you kill him? What did Nathan King do to you?"

"None of your bizz-ness, Agatha." One jerk on the rope confirmed the knot was secure. "You wouldn't understand anyway. You and your perfect little home with your long line of guests just waiting to hand over money so they can spend a few days on the river. You have a perfect life, Agatha. I wonder if you know that."

"I do now," Agatha muttered.

"And Emma, you and your savant husband, taking vacations in Texas. If that isn't putting on airs, I don't know what is. I had everything figured out, even waited for the rain so it would erase any clues. But you and Henry had to go snooping around. Well, now you're going to pay for that."

"What are you planning to do with us?" Emma's voice didn't waver at all. In fact, she sounded as if she was speaking to a wayward child.

"None of your bees-wax." Quick as a wildfire crossing a dry Texas field, Nathan's killer sprinted to the door.

Agatha couldn't make out much in the darkness of the barn. Some old hay bales were stacked against one wall. Cobwebs covered the ceiling, and something . . . something with beady eyes stared at her.

"What is that?"

"Ha. You've noticed my little friends. Don't

worry about them. Bats are nocturnal. You'll be dead long before they begin their nightly hunt." And with a last cackle, the person Agatha had thought she knew, a member of their own congregation, Nathan's killer, fled into the afternoon.

"Agatha, we have a problem."

"Yup. I don't like bats, though I am aware that they eat a lot of mosquitos and such."

"Not what I'm talking about."

"Rats? Did you see a rat?"

"Over there." Emma must have nodded toward the direction that Agatha couldn't see. She felt a tug on the rope as Emma leaned slightly forward.

"What is it?"

"A gas can."

That was when Agatha finally admitted to herself that they were in very serious trouble.

Chapter Sixteen

The first two buggies Henry and Tony checked out were a bust. The first buggy had a license plate containing the same last two numbers, but it was in pristine condition—no dents on the back at all. The second was also clearly not the one they were looking for. It sat behind an old barn, cobwebs and bird nests covering it. Plainly it had not been driven in some time.

Which left them with one possibility. Henry had heard Agatha mention Clarence Yutzy. She seemed to be on friendly terms with him. It was doubtful the man had shot young Joey or killed Nathan, but perhaps they could find a clue. Maybe he could point them to the murderer. This could be over soon, and they could all go home. It was even possible that Henry and Emma could get in some bird watching before they left for Colorado.

Henry and Tony turned into Clarence Yutzy's place.

They'd batted around possible scenarios on the drive over, but neither man had been able to come up with a reason that this investigation was pointing toward the Yutzy family. Was there a squabble between the two families? One worth killing over?

They saw only one buggy, off to the side of the barn. It was a newer model and in good condition. Still, something was off here. Henry could feel it like he could feel winter coming. After knocking on the front door, Clarence's wife directed them toward the back pasture where Clarence was mending a fence.

As they walked toward him, Henry turned up the collar on his coat. "I thought Texas was always warm. This feels more like Indiana weather, or possibly Colorado."

Tony was scanning the pasture, as if he expected a murderer to pop up from an adjacent field. "Yup. Folks say that Texas has four seasons."

"Spring, summer, fall, and winter?"

"Drought, flood, blizzard, and twister."

Henry laughed. "Let's hope we're not headed toward a blizzard."

"Or a twister. Don't like the weather? Hang around twelve hours. It's bound to change."

"Tumultuous."

"Well, sometimes it changes for the better."

Clarence greeted them, though he appeared to have no idea why they were there. After saying hello, he turned his attention back to the fence and proceeded to stretch wire around a post.

"Let me help with that." Tony steadied the post while Clarence fastened the wire.

"Should hold." Clarence wiped at sweat beading on his forehead. "What can I help you two with?"

"We have a few questions, Mr. Yutzy." Tony tugged on his ball cap. "Is there somewhere else we could talk? Somewhere out of the wind?"

"We'll try not to take too much of your time," Henry added.

Yutzy put his hands on his hips and stared down the fence line, his mouth drooping at the corners down into a frown. Apparently he'd planned to stand out in the weather and continue working on the fence, but he motioned back toward the small cluster of buildings—a nice sized farmhouse, what looked like a *Dawdi Haus*, a large barn, and several smaller out buildings.

They never actually made it into the barn, but they did shelter on the south side. Once they were out of the wind, the weather wasn't nearly as intolerable. It occurred to Henry that this community had picked a good spot to settle. Surrounded by hills, fertile fields and small towns, it was exactly what Plain people sought in an area. Other than the murders . . .

Tony jumped right to the point. "I suppose you've heard that we're looking into Nathan's murder."

"Someone might have mentioned it."

"And you know about Henry's drawings?"

One curt nod was the only answer they

received. Henry understood that they'd have to win this man over if they wanted to receive any answers. Unless he was the killer, in which case winning him over probably wouldn't be possible.

"My wife, Emma, and I came to Texas to try the fishing." Henry smiled and scratched at his left eyebrow. "Didn't expect to be a witness in a murder."

"But you didn't witness it. Did you? Actually you arrived after the event, and it's not like this . . . this gift of yours allows you to see into the past." Yutzy pulled at his shirt, then crossed his arms, then stuck his hands in the pockets of his coat.

Henry glanced at Tony. Clarence Yutzy was obviously nervous about something.

Possibly it was time for Henry to slip into his role as a bishop. Maybe that was why *Gotte* had put him in this place, at this particular time—so that he could help this man who was so obviously struggling.

"Life often gives us something we don't want. *Ya*? In the book of Corinthians, Paul tells us that we may be *hard pressed on every side,* but we won't be crushed. We won't be destroyed."

Yutzy closed his eyes, then sank onto a bench against the barn's wall. "Are you really a bishop?"

"I am. Our community is in Monte Vista, Colorado. It's small—like yours."

Yutzy seemed to consider that, then nodded. "And this drawing ability of yours . . . it's something you didn't want?"

"What I didn't want was to get hit in the head by a ball my friend Atlee smashed with his bat. Should have been a home run. Instead, it stopped here." Henry tapped the side of his head. "The things that came after were all a result of that moment."

When Yutzy didn't respond to that, he added, "And I have to think that . . . you know . . . *Gotte* didn't have His attention turned elsewhere during that moment. He wasn't simply distracted by something else, and it happened by accident."

"*Gotte* meant for you to be hit in the head with a baseball? To suffer a brain injury?"

Henry shrugged, then smiled. *"All things work together for the good . . . ya?"*

"So I've always heard, but there are days I wonder." Yutzy's voice became choked with emotion. "Everything is . . . it's out of hand. I don't know how we reached this point. I don't know what I could have done differently."

Tony cleared his throat. "The reason we're here, Mr. Yutzy, is because we think you know something about Nathan's murder. No one is accusing you, and we're not officially working for the police."

"Then why are you involved?" Irritation once again won out over any need to unburden himself. "Why can't you just let it be?"

"Because my friend, Agatha, needs my help. We think that whoever killed Nathan might not be done. I'm worried that next the killer will set his or her sights on Agatha. I can't let that happen. Could you?"

Yutzy waved the question away, as if it were no more than a pesky fly. "Whoever killed Nathan King—I think it was a one-time thing. I think it was an accident."

"And what about Joey Troyer?" Henry knew word would have already reached the entire community about the attack on Joey. Of course they didn't know that his name was actually Joey Smith or that he lived in Dallas and wasn't Amish. Those details would take a while longer to make the rounds.

"It's true then . . . he was shot?"

"Looks like it was with the same caliber weapon." Tony sat beside Yutzy on the bench. "Joey's going to be okay, because we found him in time. But the next person might not be. Whoever is doing this . . . they're feeling cornered. When killers feel cornered, they tend to kill again."

"But what if the person isn't a killer?" Yutzy shot to his feet. "What if it's just . . . someone who is confused?"

Which to Henry seemed like a mighty strange thing to say. It made him wonder. Was it possible that Clarence Yutzy knew the identity of the killer?

Chapter Seventeen

Tony didn't back off just because Yutzy seemed irritated. Henry expected the detective in the man was in charge now. He reminded Henry of his little beagle Lexi. Tony Vargas had caught the scent he was seeking, and now he was on point and ready to give chase.

"Someone saw your buggy near Agatha's barn at the time that Nathan was shot. Can you explain that?"

"*Nein.* I cannot."

Henry thought Yutzy might be about to bolt. He nodded to Tony, indicating for the man to back down a little. Tony dropped his gaze to the ground, shook his head in frustration and stepped away.

"Tell me what's on your heart, Clarence." Henry had been a bishop for a very long time. He knew when someone was struggling emotionally, and the man standing in front of him was carrying a heavy burden for sure and certain. "If you'd like we can call for your bishop to join us, but you need to tell us what's going on. You need to let us help."

"Jonas Schrock is a *gut* man—a *gut* bishop, but

he's tried to help in this situation to no avail."

"What situation?"

"My *schweschder*." As the word *schweschder* slipped from his lips, Yutzy deflated like a balloon that couldn't hold itself up without air. "Jonas has been trying to help me with her for some time, and honestly we haven't made any headway. She's simply—well, she's difficult to live with."

"Okay." Henry nodded as if that made sense, though it didn't. What did Clarence's *schweschder* have to do with Nathan's murder?

"I'm not saying that Eunice had anything to do with Nathan's murder," he clarified, as if he could read Henry's mind. "But her reaction to his death . . . it just isn't normal. It isn't right."

He hopped up and began pacing in front of them, the story spilling out like water breaching a dam. "They went out together about six months ago. I wouldn't even call it courting, because it never became that serious. Eunice turned forty-one earlier this year, and maybe that hit her hard. Either way, suddenly she was agreeable to dating. She even asked my *fraa* to help her arrange an outing with someone."

"And your wife arranged for her to date Nathan King?"

"*Ya*. They went out two . . . no, three times. Eunice became more sullen and contrary with each date. Finally Nathan came to me and said that he was sorry but it wasn't going to work."

"How did you respond to that?" Tony asked.

"I thanked him for being honest and forthright. Trust me, I know how difficult Eunice can be." He stared off across the hills, suddenly lost in another time. "Yesterday my *fraa* found this in Eunice's bureau drawer. She wasn't snooping mind you, only putting away her clothes."

Yutzy reached into his pocket and pulled out a broken chain. On the end of it was some sort of whistle.

"What is that?" Tony asked.

"Something Nathan wore. He always had it on when I saw him. It's a . . . you know . . . silent whistle. Helped to call up the goats when he needed to move them or load them." He turned it over in his hand. "It's not like it's jewelry. We don't wear any of that, not even a wedding band, but this was for Nathan's work. I just don't understand why she stole it . . . why she kept it."

"Can we have that?" Tony patted his pockets, then glanced at Henry.

He didn't have to say what they were both thinking. The whistle and chain were part of the case now. They wouldn't want to be adding to the fingerprints on it. Henry pulled out a handkerchief, and Yutzy dropped the item on top of it. Tony wrapped it up and put it in his pocket.

"Eunice wasn't always like she is now. When she was a young thing, she'd run about and play

234

with others like any normal child. The trouble started in her teen years and . . . well, things got worse from there."

"Did she see a doctor?" Henry's voice was gentle. He understood that many times Plain folk were hesitant to approach *Englisch* professionals, especially if the problem was related to mental or emotional health. They felt it was the family's place to love and care for such individuals, and only in the most severe cases did they seek medical intervention.

"My parents finally agreed to take her to a special doctor who diagnosed her with schizophrenia. The doctor put her on several medications and for a while she was better."

"But then she stopped taking them."

It was an old story, one that always broke Henry's heart. And such things didn't only occur in Amish families. When he'd taken one parishioner into a mental health facility, the doctor had explained that it was a vicious cycle for many mental health patients. They would reach a low point, seek help, receive a thorough medical work-up, and be prescribed counseling and medication. The two things worked, usually so well that the person stopped one or both, at which point they'd begin to slide back down into the pit of mental illness.

"*Ya*. We didn't know at first. She was *gut* at pretending, at hiding the medication." Now he turned to look at Henry. "I'd hoped that moving here . . . that a change of scenery might help."

"I'm truly sorry for what you're going through. You're not the first family I've counseled with these sorts of problems."

Tony pulled out his phone, glanced at it, then shook his head once and stuck it back in his pocket. "So her reaction to Nathan's death was unusual?"

"Worse than that," Clarence admitted. "She laughed about it. She was almost giddy. That's why I didn't want her going to the funeral. Then she snuck in, and I'm sure you either heard about or saw what happened. Goats everywhere. It was quite the mess."

Henry stepped forward, put his hands on the man's shoulders and waited until Yutzy raised his gaze. "*Gotte* loves you, Clarence. He loves you and your *fraa*, your *kinner* and *grandkinner*, and your *schweschder* Eunice. I can't tell you what will solve this problem, but I can tell you that you don't need to be ashamed of it."

Tears slid down Clarence's leathery cheeks. He nodded, as if he'd hoped as much but been afraid to believe it.

"I'll admit we haven't reacted well. It's easier to avoid others, stay here on the farm, try to deal with it ourselves. But honestly, Eunice has become too much for us to handle. Her illness, it's beyond me."

"We're all injured in one way or another. That's a side effect of going through this life; but we're all blessed too." Henry clapped his hands together and smiled. "Where Is Eunice? I would be happy to speak with her."

Clarence shook his head. "Off. She goes off a lot lately."

"Off where? And how?"

"She takes the older buggy usually. It's smaller, so we rarely use it for the family. Plus it's quite dented up. Sometimes she rides an old bike around town. Often she loads the bike onto the back of the buggy. She's quite strong physically. It's only mentally and emotionally that she suffers."

Again, Henry and Tony glanced at one another.

They needed to see this bike.

They needed to question Eunice.

"I bought this old place a few miles from here. I thought my son might want it, but he moved back east. I've been meaning to clean it up and sell it, but there hasn't been time. The house is dilapidated, and the barn is falling down. I don't know why I've kept it. I guess I was dreaming that Eunice would marry, and then . . ." His words faded away, as had his dream of Eunice marrying.

"I can come back tomorrow if you like, and we can speak more of this. Emma and I are here until Monday. When Eunice comes home, call Agatha's and leave a message."

237

Clarence nodded, looking relieved at Henry's offer.

"What does she do out there?" Tony asked.

"What do you mean?"

"When she goes out to your old place . . . what does she do there?"

Now Clarence laughed, though somewhat sheepishly. "My *schweschder* has got it in her head that she's an Amish cowgirl. She wears these old boots I bought from a yard sale, and she likes to go out and lasso things."

"Lasso things?" The hairs on the back of Henry's neck pricked up.

"*Ya*. She even asked for a new rope for Christmas last year. It's a harmless hobby—she ropes bales of hay, fence posts, that sort of thing."

Henry could tell by Tony's suddenly stiff posture that he was one step ahead, but Henry caught up quickly because it made sense now.

The bits of rope on the goat's fur.

The bruise around Nathan's neck.

The missing chain and whistle.

Eunice's hobby.

Everything was falling into place. Everything except the manner of death because Nathan hadn't been killed by a rope. He'd been shot.

Clarence was still talking, his voice coming to Henry as if from a far distance. "Sometimes she even takes my old hunting rifle out and sets up cans . . . shoots at them."

Tony pulled out his phone and tapped on the screen until he'd pulled up the maps program. "Show me. Show me where your place is."

And then they were running toward the truck, leaving Clarence standing there with his mouth hung open and a look of utter confusion on his face.

Henry turned and hurried back to the man. "Go to the phone shack. Call Jonas and ask him to come here, to wait with you. We'll be in touch as soon as we know something."

"Is Eunice in trouble?"

"Maybe. I don't know, but we'll find out, and we'll be in touch as soon as we know something."

He could tell the man had more questions, but Tony had already started the truck. Henry jogged back to him and climbed into the vehicle as Tony's phone buzzed. Tony answered it, his jaw clenching even as his grip on the wheel tightened. They were speeding down the lane now, throwing white rock and raising a cloud of dust.

"They went where? . . . How long ago? . . . Call the police, Gina. Tell them everything you told me. Tell them to send a squad car and that the suspect might be mentally unstable." At this point he swerved out onto the blacktop road. "Tell them she might be mentally unstable, that she's a diagnosed schizophrenic off her meds. Tell them to hurry."

He ended the call and said the last words Henry wanted to hear. "Agatha received a note. It gave a location and told her to be there within the hour if she wanted to know who had killed Nathan King. She and Emma left forty-five minutes ago."

"And the place?"

"Old farm on the west side of town." Tony punched the accelerator. "Clarence Yutzy's place."

Chapter Eighteen

A gatha and Emma tried in vain to wiggle out of Eunice's lasso.

"The woman knows how to tie a rope," Emma muttered.

"Indeed she does. But what does she have planned for us?"

Emma thought she'd been whispering, but Eunice stepped into the room and shrieked, "Wouldn't you like to know?"

Before Agatha could answer, she snatched up the gas can and darted back out quick as two shakes from a duck's tail.

"What's she going to do with that gas can?" Emma squirmed with renewed vigor.

It didn't help.

Each time either of them moved it only tightened the rope on the other. Agatha was already losing the feeling in her arms and fingers. How long had they been sitting there? Had Gina managed to get in contact with Tony and Henry? And when were those bats going to stop sleeping and start hunting? Because Agatha did not intend to be around when that happened.

She paused in her squirming to stare up at the

241

bats. "I think one just blinked at me, or nodded, or maybe it was simply thinking I look juicy."

"Stop worrying about those bats and think of a way to get out of these knots."

Which was undoubtedly what she should do, but suddenly Agatha was besieged by images of having her hands cuffed in front of her with plastic ties, being thrown in the back of a van, Tony telling her to jump . . ." She shook her head and tried to dislodge the memories. The past wasn't what she needed to focus on now.

"Are you okay?" Emma asked.

"*Ya*. Mostly. You?"

"My right shoulder hurts, but other than that . . ."

Then three things happened nearly simultaneously.

First, Agatha suddenly noticed the acrid smell of smoke.

Second, the bats startled, swooped, and with a great flurry of little bat wings they darted out of the barn.

And third and most distressing, Eunice stuck her head back into their room. "Can't stay."

"Eunice, stop this right now." Agatha aimed for her most serious grandmotherly tone. "You don't want to kill us. Come over here and undo these ropes."

"Sorry. Can't."

"What do you mean you can't?" Emma's patience had plainly snapped.

"I'm out of here . . . double quick . . . fast as a lightning bolt . . . like an arrow from a bow."

And then she was gone.

"There's something wrong with Eunice." Emma's voice was grim, but she wasn't panicked.

"She's right about one thing, though. She can't stay and neither should we. This place is about to go up like a carefully constructed bonfire."

"How are we supposed to leave?"

Which was a very good question, made more pressing by the increased smell of fire, tendrils of smoke, and tiny flames coming from the other side of the wall where Eunice had been. What had she done? Did she actually mean to kill them?

The fire Eunice had obviously set crept under the wall separating the two rooms, snaked across the floor and reached the bales of hay on the far side of the room, which caused flames to spit, crackle, and then quickly spread.

Agatha had no intention of dying in a fire. She was going to Shipshe for vacation. She was going to see her grandchildren, and she had a B&B to run, and there were things she wanted to say to Tony. "We need to stand up."

"What?"

"Stand up. Push with your back and your feet on three. One, two, three!"

Emma grunted and Agatha pushed with all of

her might. They raised up a fraction of an inch, then dropped back to the crates Eunice had insisted they sit on. The thud felt like it rattled Agatha's bones. She pushed away the pain. She could think about that later.

"Try again. Ready?"

"*Ya*. We can do this."

This time they made it all the way up, then fell back down when both Agatha and Emma attempted to turn toward the door. Now smoke was obscuring their vision. Emma coughed, and sweat dripped down Agatha's temples. But her perspiration wasn't from the heat of the fire. She was frightened, maybe more frightened than she'd ever been.

"*Gotte*, please help us." Her chest hurt and she wondered if she was having a heart attack. "One more time, Emma. On three, and you turn toward the door. Swing to your right."

"Got it."

"One, two . . . three."

And suddenly, miraculously, they were up and moving toward the barn door. The ropes bit into Agatha's arms. The crates they had been sitting on bumped into their legs and threatened to send them sprawling. If only they could work their way free of them, they might be able to run, but there wasn't time.

And perhaps miraculously, they didn't trip, but instead inched toward the door.

The flames raced across the floor, a distant part of the roof caved in, and somewhere outside Eunice's horse gave out a frightened neigh and thundered past the barn.

Agatha coughed and fought the urge to drop down and cover her head. She couldn't drop down. They had to keep moving.

As they reached the door, she shouted, "Don't stop. Keep going, Emma. As far as you can go. We need to get clear of this fire."

They made it a dozen feet from the barn before they fell to the ground.

Tony and Henry passed Eunice on the caliche road. She was madly pumping the pedals on her old bicycle, headed down the lane, headed away from the old buildings and toward the main road. Tony braked, no doubt in order to block her path and apprehend her, but Henry shouted, "Over there!"

Henry pointed to smoke coming from an old dilapidated barn that, as they watched, burst into flames. Agatha's horse and buggy were parked a good distance from the structure, but Eunice's buggy caught fire as Tony slammed down on the accelerator. In the distance, Henry thought he saw a buggy horse galloping away.

But those things were all in his peripheral vision. The one thing he strained to see, the one thing he had to see was Agatha and Emma.

"Please, *Gotte* . . ." The words were more than a prayer, they were a plea from the very center of his heart.

Leaning forward, he saw the two women, tied up like two calves, stumbling from the structure.

Tony spied them at the same moment, accelerating and then slamming the truck to a stop a good twenty feet away. Both men were out of the vehicle the second he jammed the gearshift into park.

Henry didn't remember crossing the distance or losing his hat. One minute he was in Tony's truck and the next he was kneeling beside Emma and Agatha. Tony had pulled out his pocketknife and was attempting to saw through the nylon rope. Henry stuck his fingers between two coils and forced them apart, tearing the skin from his fingertips as he did so.

And then the knife did its work.

The rope slipped away.

The women fell onto the ground.

"We need to get behind the truck," Tony hollered.

Henry realized that the fire was roaring now. The wind had whipped it to a fury and the old wood provided ample fuel. He helped Emma to her feet as Tony helped Agatha, and then they were running toward the truck.

"To the far side," Tony shouted.

As they collapsed onto the ground behind the

truck there was a whoosh and a boom and pieces of old wood flew into the air and flopped onto the dirt. One or two pieces of flaming debris pinged the other side of Tony's truck.

Agatha shouted and covered her head with her arms.

Emma threw herself into Henry's arms.

And then, from a distance, they heard the sound of sirens.

"The police?" Emma asked.

"And hopefully a fire truck." Tony stood and peeked over the hood of the truck. "Clarence's horse looks fine—made it to the boundary fence."

"What about Doc?" Agatha popped up beside him.

"Your horse is good. Smart of you to park it so far away from the structure."

"I didn't know Eunice was going to set the place on fire, but I wanted a safe distance between her and my horse."

"What happened?" Henry asked. "How did . . . how did you end up trussed like a couple of calves?"

Agatha gave them the short version with Emma chiming in with occasional details like Agatha's fear of bats.

Crossing her arms across her middle, Agatha defended herself with the claim that her fear was "perfectly normal."

"We need to get you a bat box." Tony smiled and clumsily patted her shoulder.

"Why would I want a bat box?"

"For bats. They're beneficial to have around. They eat a lot of insects."

"Uh-huh. Let me think about it."

Henry heard all this, but his thoughts had drifted to encompass all that he was seeing. He had explained many times that his subconscious mind was what saw every minute detail, not his conscious mind. But something about drawing—about embracing his gift—had caused his conscious mind to become more aware of things, especially during incidents that were emotionally stuffed and brimming over.

And in that moment, he was almost painfully aware of every detail.

The fire raging in the background.

The emergency personnel speeding toward them.

Agatha smiling up at Tony, and the way he looked back at her with real affection.

And brighter and more vivid than any of those things—Emma. Emma shaking slightly. Emma tucking a loose lock of hair into her *kapp* and then staring at her hands and attempting to brush the soot from them, wiping her palms against the fabric of her dress. Emma standing so close to him that it seemed as if their hearts beat in rhythm with one another. Emma smelling of smoke and under that something more familiar and comforting—baking and knitting and soap mixing into the very essence of who she was. He saw in her eyes the fear and the relief and the love that she felt for him.

And Henry Lapp, who considered himself a very grounded and practical person, had to fight the urge to fall onto his knees and thank the Lord for this life, for these people, and for the woman who was by his side every day.

Instead, he sent up a silent prayer to his Heavenly Father and slipped his arms around Emma. "You frightened me," he whispered.

"I frightened myself."

"That was entirely too close."

"Agreed." Emma stood on tiptoe and kissed him on the cheek, then her expression grew suddenly serious. "So Eunice did it? She actually killed Nathan?"

And then it was Henry and Tony's turn to explain—about Clarence, about Eunice's history of mental illness, and about her delusions that she was an Amish cowgirl.

"Certainly explains her skill with a rope," Agatha muttered.

Before they could piece together the final details of the mystery, all conversation stopped because emergency personnel were crowding around them, insisting on administering aid to Emma and Agatha. Help had arrived, and Henry was very glad to see them.

Chapter Nineteen

Two days later, Tony offered to drive Henry and Emma to San Antonio to catch their bus. Agatha went along, happy to be with friends, happy to have a day away. She felt inexplicably light. How good and right it was to simply be able to enjoy life, and to not be troubled by dark matters such as murder.

They left early and travelled the back roads to show Henry and Emma more of the Hill Country. They cruised through Kerrville, then slowed as they passed the small downtown of Bandera and finally turned east through Helotes and into the sprawl of San Antonio. Usually Agatha preferred the short distance and slow speed of a buggy ride, but on this day she found herself sticking her hand out the window like a pup on a road trip.

When they'd made their way through the traffic and into downtown, Tony looked at his watch. "We still have over an hour before your bus departs. Mind if I take you to a favorite spot? We can have a late breakfast or early lunch."

"Sounds like a great idea," Emma said. "Gina made sandwiches for us to eat on the bus for our dinner, and then it's another year of cooking for me. Come to think of it, I rather miss cooking."

Henry laughed. "Another benefit of vacation—makes you appreciate home, both the chores and the familiarity of it."

Tony pulled into the parking area for La Panaderia.

"Smells *gut* even from here."

"And it tastes even better." Before they went inside, Tony explained a little of the history of the place. "Jose and David opened up this bakery and café only a few years ago. The interesting thing is that they learned to bake from their *madre*. *Doña* Josefina sold fresh baked bread on the streets of Mexico City. She was quite prosperous, and they learned from her success, then brought their business to Texas."

"So it's a family enterprise." Emma smiled. "That's nice."

"Just wait until you taste it."

They feasted on breakfast sandwiches made of ham, Swiss cheese, eggs and avocado, served on fresh croissants with a side of black beans. Strong black coffee and dessert rounded out the meal—one bear claw, an *oreja*, a small monkey bread, and a *peineta*. They put all four desserts in the middle of the table and took a bite of each.

"I'm going to sleep on the bus," Henry predicted.

"And I'll knit. We're as full as bugs in a rug. *Danki*, Tony. It's been a fine end to our trip."

251

Henry nodded in agreement. "Agatha, I can't help but believe *Gotte* caused our paths to cross."

"Maybe so." Agatha beamed at the two of them. "I didn't expect to have an Amish bishop and savant dropped into my B&B, but you, your wife, and your talents sure came in handy. We couldn't have solved the murder without you."

"Speaking of murder . . . have you had any updates on Eunice?"

Tony nodded. "Let me refill our coffee cups. Then I'll tell you all I know."

What he knew was a lot. Eunice had felt spurned by Nathan. She'd obsessed over their relationship and finally begun to follow him. When he ignored her, or told her to go home—and that happened on more than one occasion—she became angry.

"Angry and desperate are a bad combination," Agatha noted.

"Indeed. On the afternoon of November third, Eunice drove her brother's buggy to the old bridge and parked it on the side of the road. Offloading her bike, she travelled back to where Nathan's goats were foraging."

"Across from the B&B." Emma seemed as caught up as Agatha was.

Hearing Tony lay out the details of the case was like reaching the conclusion of a novel—only this story involved real people, real lives, and real tragedy.

"As we suspected from your drawings, Eunice managed to get his attention by lassoing one of the goats. When Nathan came to rescue it, they argued. Eunice shot him, then yanked off and pocketed the whistle he wore on the chain around his neck."

"Which caused the bruising," Henry said.

"Yup. And it also explains the partial boot print. She didn't have to step closer to kill him, but she did have to stand over his body in order to retrieve the necklace."

"What was the argument about?" Agatha shook her head in disbelief. "Didn't Nathan realize that she was dangerous?"

"We don't know much about the details of what was said between the two. Eunice still refuses to explain exactly what pushed her over the edge."

"Maybe she doesn't know." Henry stared out the window for a moment, then turned his attention back to his friends. "Maybe she can't explain it even to herself."

"That's certainly possible. We do know that she was carrying Clarence's old rifle, so she anticipated using it. We don't know if she actually set out that day planning to kill Nathan, but there are grounds for premeditation. The prosecution will be able to charge her with first degree murder if and when she's deemed competent to stand trial."

Agatha sat up straighter. What Eunice had done

was wrong, but putting her in jail for the rest of her life wouldn't right that wrong. "Is that a possibility . . . her standing trial for murder?"

"It's doubtful. Texas allows an insanity defense. According to the M'Naghten rule, a defendant who is unable to distinguish between right and wrong may be found not guilty by reason of insanity."

"To me she seemed like a child—an angry one at times, to be sure, but still a child."

"And there's little doubt that she was unable to control her impulses, given she was not taking her medication and her previous diagnosis of schizophrenia."

"So she walks free?" Emma shook her head. "She doesn't belong in jail, but I'm not sure that Clarence can handle her."

"She'll be sent somewhere that she can receive psychiatric care. Your bishop . . ." Tony let his gaze rest on Agatha for a moment.

His attention caused her pulse to jump, but she rather liked it.

"Jonas."

"Right. He's been in touch with a group of Mennonites who run a mental health center. It'll be a little bit of a drive for Clarence to visit her, but they can provide the care Eunice needs. They'll also keep a close eye on her. Hopefully, with time, she'll eventually be able to return home."

"And Joey?" Agatha asked. "Why did she shoot Joey?"

"Eunice hid across the road after the shooting. When Joey fled the scene, she saw him. After that, it was simply a matter of following him until he was alone."

"My barn."

"Yup. Your barn."

Which seemed to sum up the case.

Tony insisted on paying for their meal. They thanked the waitress and stepped out into a November day that was cold but sunny and startling in its beauty. Hanging baskets of flowers adorned storefronts, and as they walked toward the bus station, they paused to look down on the San Antonio River. Boats of tourists floated past them, and along the river walk restaurants boasted patio tables with brightly colored umbrellas.

"Looks like an oasis," Henry said.

"Something we can all use from time to time." Emma reached for her husband's hand and smiled at him.

Agatha liked that about them—many Amish still held to the old ways, refusing to show any type of affection in public. Emma and Henry had found each other late in life, and they weren't going to hold back on how they felt because of such traditions.

At the station, Agatha pulled Emma into a

hug. "You're welcome to come back any time."

"And you could come visit us in Monte Vista. It's beautiful there. You and Tony should both come. It would be a nice vacation for you."

"I just might take you up on it." Agatha rather liked the idea of driving with Tony through the Colorado mountains, and she'd also have a chance to see a lot of Texas just trying to get out of it.

When she said goodbye to Henry, he held her hand in his and said, "*Gotte* bless you, Agatha. What you're doing here . . . providing a haven of rest for weary people . . . it's *Gotte*'s work."

His words touched her heart. She'd made a vow when she'd first moved to Texas. In fact, those very words, *haven of rest,* were etched on a bronze plaque that was tucked into her garden, honoring the memory of her *bruder.* Below that line was another that read *May God's peace fill your soul.*

She supposed those two lines summed up her mission statement for her B&B, but few guests paused long enough to read the words on the plaque. Fewer still guessed how deep their meaning ran for her. Tears pricked her eyes, but she managed a strangled "*Danki.*"

"I have something for you." He removed a postcard-sized piece of paper from his shirt pocket.

She stared down at it, at the picture of her B&B with the Guadalupe River flowing behind it and felt tears sting her eyes. "It's beautiful, Henry."

"It's his first scenic piece," Emma explained. "He's going to do a book of them, then donate the money he earns."

"A way of using your gift," Tony said.

"Exactly."

Emma enfolded her in one last hug, and then they hurried off to catch their bus.

She and Tony waited until the bus pulled out, then they walked arm in arm back to his truck. Forty-five minutes later they'd left the bustle of San Antonio behind them.

"Henry and Emma are *gut* people," she declared.

"Salt of the earth."

"What's that?"

"You haven't heard that saying?" Tony tugged on his ball cap, then smiled at her. "My dad used to call people he liked, people who didn't stand on pretense and would help you out of a jam, salt of the earth."

"I like that."

"Yup."

"My life has certainly been interesting since I moved to Texas."

"My life has been interesting since you moved to Texas."

She turned toward him, a smile playing on her lips. Deciding she had nothing to lose, she leaned over and kissed him on the cheek.

"What did I do to deserve that?"

"Just being who you are—being the salt of the earth." She mimicked his voice and he laughed. "I wonder what's next."

"I have literally no idea."

"One thing I'm sure of . . . it's not going to involve murder."

"You're sure about that?"

"Absolutely. I'm done. No more sleuthing for me."

"Uh-huh."

"I mean it, Tony. I'm not planning anything more exciting than sitting in a kayak with you and learning to fish."

"You're not a very good fisher."

"I am, too." She knew he was teasing, but she couldn't help defending herself. "I caught those sunfish, and I didn't fall in."

"You're setting a mighty low bar."

"True."

"You squeal whenever you catch a fish."

"It's exciting."

"Exciting enough."

"Exactly." She didn't need murders or clues or investigations. All Agatha needed was the sun slanting through her kitchen window, guests to care for, good friends like Gina and Becca and

Emma, and the certainty that God had her in the palm of his hands.

Of course, having a good-looking neighbor as a best friend didn't hurt one bit.

Dedication

This book is dedicated to my friend Priscilla Wright. She's that rare kind of friend who is there for you through the good and the bad. Also she helps me pick out the perfect shade of lipstick. Priscilla, I hope you enjoyed the character that was inspired by you.

I need to again thank Beth Scott for the use of her cat Fonzi, and others from our church's ladies' group who may find their names sprinkled throughout this story. You all are a joy to be around, especially when we're drinking coffee.

As is always the case, I owe a large debt to my pre-readers, Kristy and Tracy. Love you both. Teresa, you did a fabulous job on the editing. Jenny, once again I absolutely adore the cover that you created. My family deserves a giant *thank you* for every single book I finish. You all are the best.

And a heartfelt shout-out to all my readers who over the years have asked for another book about Henry. I hope you enjoyed his return.

And finally . . . *always giving thanks to God the*

Father for everything, in the name of our Lord Jesus Christ (Ephesians 5:20).
Blessings,
Vannetta

Author's Note

There is no Plain community in Hunt, Texas, though I have no trouble picturing one there. Hunt sits squarely in the middle of the Texas Hill Country, an area growing increasingly popular, especially for folks trying to escape the fast pace and stressful life of Dallas, Houston, and San Antonio. It's a beautiful part of our state, and as you drive the twisting roads that follow the Guadalupe, you can catch a glimpse of the Texas that used to be.

I had the pleasure of conducting thorough research in the community of Hunt. Any differences from the real location were done for purposes to further my plot. Likewise, though I have visited over a dozen Amish communities, the community you read about in this book is fictional and subject to intentional discrepancies in the interest of dramatic license.

I first wrote about Bishop Henry in *What the Bishop Saw*. Accidental/acquired savant syndrome is a condition where dormant savant skills emerge after a brain injury or disease. Although it's quite rare, researchers in 2010 identified 32 individuals who displayed unusual skills in one or more of five major areas: art, musical abilities, calendar calculation, arithmetic, and spatial skills. Males with savant syndrome outnumber females by roughly six to one.

Center Point Large Print
600 Brooks Road / PO Box 1
Thorndike, ME 04986-0001 USA

(207) 568-3717

US & Canada:
1 800 929-9108
www.centerpointlargeprint.com